1920

&

The Secrets that Kept Her

1920
&
The Secrets that Kept Her

*Seventy five years of Secrets held beyond the
shores of Lake Chatuge*

Sara Hall

DEDICATION

In Honor of:
The Hayesville Historical Society

&

With love to:
Randy, Robert, Layton, Madelyn, Logan & Landon.

Elwyn, Donna, Tom & Betsy

ACKNOWLEDGEMENTS

Have you ever had a moment when you hear the name of a person and you instantly know you will have a lifelong relationship with them? That's how I met May. She has been the best friend to my mother in law, Betsy, for many years. Finally, after a visit to the local garden in downtown Hayesville, I was able to meet her- muck shoes on, and a big brimmed hat to hide her from the sun. Her infectious smile and laughter affirmed what I already knew about her, she was as good as gold. Since then, I've been able to learn more of her. May Ferguson Atkinson, holds two Master's Degrees in Education, is a Master Gardener for Clay County NC, and is the Editor of this book. She has been of great help through the process of writing this book, for which I am so thankful.

To Sandy Zimmerman, for extending her knowledge about the history of Hayesville, and her unfailing determination to save a beautiful historic courthouse.

To Betsy Hall, thank you for the kitchen island time where i read to you, and for the encouragement you have provided. I wouldn't have been able to do this without you.

To Randy, your constant love has kept this dream alive. Thank you for believing in me! I love you!

Forward

1920 & The Secrets that Kept Her, began in an antique store. I found a photo of a regal old man, and a few intriguing post cards that dropped a story right in my lap. I told my husband, Randy, of the book idea, and he told me to go for it. I began to write out my ideas in a notebook and collect a few other pictures over the coming weeks. Around Thanksgiving, we took a trip to Hayesville, and over a cup of coffee early one morning, I pulled out the notebook, photographs, and my laptop to begin writing this book. I knew very little of Hayesville's history but I wanted to incorporate it into the book. Betsy, my mother in aw took me downtown to show me the old jail, the courthouse, the town square, and the historical society.

The historical facts based in the book were collected from the historical society over several visits and lots of research.

The photographs helped me to create the characters. Some of the photos are from the era, others are just interesting, and provided me with the idea of character or a bit of a storyline. I hope that having them displayed will provide you with the understanding of the character's demeanor and a visual aide through the book.

The book took a little over two years to write, start to finish.

If you are writing, don't give up. It is worth it in the end.

Chapter One

The Phone Call

As days go this was a normal one for Edmund; filing papers at the courthouse in Raleigh, North Carolina, for divorce after divorce. He was the lead paralegal at Halstead Law, a large firm in the triangle area. Edmund kept himself busy with work to keep his mind off of life. His father had passed away a year ago tomorrow. He was thankful that it was almost over. The year of probate was draining on him, physically and financially.

His father, Porter, was the only family he had ever had. His dementia had truly taken his father years before his peaceful passing; yet, his poor body remained stuck in a time warp of a far-gone forgotten era.

Porter Monroe Wise

This was the last chapter before he felt like he could move on and finally be himself, not the caretaker of a demented soul who was stuck somewhere in the 1940s. Tomorrow he would meet with his father's attorney, Mr. Jackson. They would go to the courthouse one last time.

"Halstead Law, this is Edmund," he said.

"Edmund, it's Mr. Jackson. We need to talk before you come tomorrow. Do you have a few minutes?"
With a heavy sigh he said sure, knowing he really didn't have an option.

Stanley Albert Jackson

Mr. Jackson was the only estate attorney from Clay County. Of course that meant that he was the man that was handling his father's estate. Mr. Jackson was left in control of his father's estate for the year of probate. Edmund would never admit it, but he was jealous of all the things Mr. Jackson was left in control of. He could only sit back and watch in agony as the casket was picked, the service was planned, and the final details were completed with no say so from the only living family member, himself.

"I know you don't think highly of your father's decision to allow me to have control over everything, and honestly, I'm ready for you to take control of this next week. He was as anal in life as he was in his final wishes, but he was protecting you. I know you don't understand that," Jackson said.

"I'm thirty-five. I think I do understand. He never cared for my decisions in life, so why would he trust me to take care of anything after his death? Either way, why he wouldn't let me have any say still boils my blood, I may never have been able to forgive him for how he treated me as a child. Not that it matters, he's dead. So, why are you calling? I've already got everything ready to head that way to be ready for tomorrow," Edmund said begrudgingly.

He knew nothing of his father's estate. Porter Monroe Wise left Stanley Albert Jackson in control. He knew that there was enough money for his father to be taken care of. Before his dementia took his faculties, full legal power of attorney was given to Jackson. No discussion, no options, no whys or why nots. It just was.

"Listen, It's not as you think. Your dad and I have history. He wanted that history to end," Jackson said.

14

"Yeah, I know, prohibition, crazy mountain talk and a life in a different era. I heard it all through his years and years of mindless conversation. I left Clay County as soon as I could. I have no desire to come back. Once I walk out of the courthouse tomorrow my life's in Raleigh. A life where no one knows the Wise name."

"It's not like you think. Listen, you need to take a few days off. One day isn't going to be enough. I know you two were never close, but I hope you'll get some answers over the next few days. I've already talked to the attorney you work for there in Raleigh. She said you can stay a few days. Estates are hard. Trust me," Jackson said to Edmund, defending his actions.

Infuriated, Edmund hung up the phone. How could Jackson just 'talk' to his boss? Does he know it's hard enough to keep a job in Raleigh on a regular day? Paralegals are a dime a dozen in this county, and he didn't want to just be a number.

Elaine walked by, trying not to stare. "Have fun on vacation," she said.

Elaine, Administrative Assistant at Halstead Law

Elaine was the administrative assistant who was a pain in the side of everyone. Her short pale frame scurried around the office seemingly knowing too much of the personal lives of everyone who worked there. When Edmund would describe her he would say she has long hair, usually in a bun pinned tightly to her head, accented her thin lips and long nose. He always thought that fit her personality.

She kissed up to the attorney in charge, and always knew everything (whether she did or not).
"Lisa wants to talk to you before you leave. She's got a five minute break now so you should go on in."

He just had to file papers for one more case.. He slammed it on his desk and headed in for what he was sure was going to be a tongue lashing.

Edmund Ross Wise

Edmund had always considered himself average. He never saw what others saw in his appearance. All he saw was the resemblance of a man he barely knew. His lack of self confidence made him shy and reserved. His bold blue eyes and dark brown hair always received stares and blushed smiles from women around town. At right around six feet tall he was hard to miss in a crowd, and that's why he avoided them as much as possible. He kept to himself, ran a few miles a day to keep in shape, and never went out. He knew he wasn't worthy of the companionship of which he often dreamt.

Lisa Halstead, Attorney

Lisa was finishing a call as he closed her office door. She turned around from looking at her panoramic view of downtown Raleigh to face Edmund. Edmund wore his embarrassment on his face. He took a deep breath, then began his apology.

"Listen, Lisa I'm sorry about...,"

"About Jackson calling?" she interrupted him mid thought.

"Jackson knows what he's doing. His family has been in the estate office of Clay County for as far back as records go. I trust him. If you are going to need a few days to clear all of this up, you are going to need a few days. Better to only go once than to have to go back a few times, right? That drive is killer long, and you need to get it finished. Now while you are gone, I've hired a temp to keep your desk moving. Come back when you can. You can work from there if you need to. If there is something you need, call. I know I'm your boss, but after 10 years I do consider you a friend."

With that, her phone rang and she was off to the races again. He quietly left and closed the door, more confused than he was before.

Why was she being so nice? What did Jackson say to her?

As he composed himself he began to have all of the feelings of hate and anger he tried to bury so many years ago. The relationship with his father was staggered to say the least, but he was the last of his line. His father was in and out of his life as his mother died when he was seven. Now that his father was dead it was really just him.

After his mother's death his father was never the same. The once calm and witty man was a mere shell of anger and pain. Edmund seemingly raised himself the best he could until he was eighteen. After high school graduation he enlisted, and stayed as far away as possible. After a training accident at Fort Hood he came to Raleigh and finished what education he had at night. He found the paralegal position with Halstead Law shortly after Lisa took over the firm from her father. It had been the only steady thing in his life for as long as he could remember.

By the time he made it back to his desk, Elaine had his last file in her hands. "I thought you were leaving," Elaine said with a smirk.
"Well, I guess I am now," Edmund smarted back.

He already had his bag in the car since he was prepared to head west after work. He had hoped to be gone by 4:45 to beat the rush hour traffic, but 2:15 would put him well ahead of schedule. Since he apparently was going to be there for more than a night, he decided to stop by his apartment to pick up a few more changes of clothes. It wasn't like he had a difficult time to decide what to take. His closet was just a few pieces of each item he needed. He didn't have sophisticated tastes. Just a simple white shirt, occasionally blue and black suits and simple ties to fulfill the daily office attire for the law firm. He picked up a few jeans and a sweater he had tucked away. The weather in Hayesville always depended on the wind and the mountains. One side of the mountain could be covered in snow, while the next valley had little more than a spit of rain. At least he would be prepared.

"Last time, Dad. Last time," Edmund said as he locked the door to his apartment and headed to the car.

It took anywhere from five to six hours to get to Hayesville from Raleigh depending on two things: weather and traffic. It was clear and no rain was in the forecast, so he hoped it would be close to five hours of mindless driving.

The drive was just as he expected, empty roads past Greensboro, few State Troopers, and rolling hills ahead. He tried not to think about tomorrow, but once he got to Black Mountain and the curves began to fill his windshield a few tears ran down his cheeks. No matter how angry he was this was for his dad.

As he neared the iced over pass just past Franklin he slowed his pace from the speed of lightening to the speed of molasses. He wanted to remember the good things about the North Carolina Mountains -it's beauty, even at night the frozen pass was one of them. The shadows of the mountains hit portions of the night sky, but the stars stood out clearer than he could ever see them in Raleigh. In a moment of child likeness he began to look for the 'beacon'. It was really just a house on the top of a mountain, but he always imagined it as a mountain lighthouse of sorts. You could see it for miles on a clear night. When it came into view he knew he was getting close, and began to look for the turn to his home away from home.

Leola's Bed & Breakfast

It was a little more expensive than what most would pay for a one-bedroom motel room, but the cooking was worth it. The last turn took him through some of the best curves in the county, and he could see the smoke from the fireplace as he pulled in the drive.

Leola met him on the porch, "I wasn't expecting you this early! Good thing I fixed an extra portion!"

"Pastry?" Edmund asked.

"Of course!" She answered, "Only the best in Clay County for my long lost city slicker, and maybe just a little apple cobbler too. Well, don't be a stranger, come on in!"

The stress of Raleigh and the long drive melted as the smells from the kitchen greeted him in the front parlor. He sat his bags down and started to remove his coat as Leola disappeared around the corner.

"Leola?" Edmund called.

"In the kitchen!" She answered.

"I'm gonna be here for an extra day or so. If that's a problem I'll get a room up the road after tomorrow."

"Don't be silly! I haven't been full since 1991. And besides, I've always got room for you. I only have one other person coming in this week, and that's not for a few days." she said.

"My normal room?" Edmund asked.

"Of course!" Leola answered.

He climbed the stairs and opened the first door on the right. He had always requested this room every time he had to come to Clay County. The room had a picturesque view of the mountains, and old hand carved wooden floors that creaked as you neared the fire place. The freshly laundered linens on the antique full sized bed and oversized pillows beckoned to him -'food first' he thought, then sleep.

Leola, Bed & Breakfast Owner

Leola's pastry was as golden as she was. Her smile lit up a room, and her bubbly, larger than life personality filled the little bed and breakfast she called home. Leola has been a staple in the Hayesville community for as far as he could remember. Her home had been opened to others throughout the years that never really had a place to call home. Leola survived a tough marriage when she was much younger. No one ever discussed her husband after he took his own life, but that didn't stop Leola from being the bold woman she was. She was refined by the fire, and made it her passion to help others when they couldn't help themselves. She never had a lot, but she always had enough to get by. She never let the struggles she had change who she was for the worse, only for the better.

Edmund was certain this was as close to his mother as he could remember- full of love and life. He soaked up every moment he could with her, she may not have been his mother, but she wasn't off by far. The apple cobbler and large glass of milk was just what he needed before bed. He was certain if his mother was still alive that this is what her food would taste like. He tucked himself in shortly after nine. The morning and all it would bring with it would be here before he knew it.

Chapter Two

The Formality

Jackson paced from his desk to the front door of his firm sipping his black coffee from the same cup he'd been drinking from for sixty years. He had made it to his office and had straightened his pens for the fifth time in ten minutes when he heard the bell ring on the front door.

"Just like we planned, Porter," he said under his breath. He cleared his throat and made his way up to the lobby to greet the long lost last Wise . Today was the day, and he was more nervous about it than he was about having to manage his best friend's estate for the last 365 days.

"Edmund Ross!" Jackson yelled as he reached out for a hug, but was only greeted with a firm handshake.

"Edmund, I go by Edmund, Sir. I haven't been called that in a long, long time. It's great to see you, Mr. Jackson."

"What time do we need to be at the courthouse?" Edmund cut him off to get to the point.

"Just like your father, straight to business," Jackson began. "Come, sit, let's talk."

Edmund sat in what was obviously an old leather wingback chair that had rarely been used. As he settled in he noticed the stress in the face of Mr. Jackson. He noticed people's faces, he made sure to look and read people .It had always been one thing he was able to pick up on.

Jackson opened his desk drawer with a slight hesitation and a bit of anxiousness, and there sat the sealed envelope labeled with Edmund's name. He took a deep breath knowing this envelope would change Clay County history. He kept his word, even through death, and seventy five years of secrets. He grasped the envelope and slid it in front of Edmund.

"What's this?" Edmund inquired.

"This, is why your father, asked me to handle the estate. If I had gone first my wife would have received verbatim an exact copy. The night your father died I burned my copy. I sat in this office, lit my cigar, and watched it slowly burn into a pile of ashes. I could stand it no longer. I know you are going to have a lot of questions, but please. Don't open it until we have finished up in court. Then we can come back here and talk about the details of the letter."

Edmund's rage and frustration boiled over the hundred-year-old desk. Rightfully so, Jackson received every bit of fury that was thrown at him.

"Mr. Jackson, you are talking in circles. Should I trust what you have done with my father's estate? Is there even anything left for me? I've spent a small fortune in gas and bed and breakfast bills driving here over the last several years. I have not received one red cent coming to help since my father left you in charge of everything. If there is nothing there I will file charges of misconduct, and breach of trust with the North Carolina Bar Association as soon as I return to Raleigh. You best believe that."

"Edmund Ross Wise, I've kept a record of every penny over the last 15 years. I know where every cent has gone. I know the interest that has added up every month, Interest that I never touched except for the expenses of Porter. You are entitled to every penny that is left after the estate is closed. Trust me, I want nothing more than to sign the registry over to you. There's a lot that your father buried, and kept from you. Things he didn't want to talk about because he wanted to keep you safe. He knew you wouldn't understand that he just wanted to keep you from it all," Jackson spat back at Edmund.

"If you are talking about the same old stories I've always heard, how my father was a moonshiner, was the closest thing Clay County came to a racecar driver, I've heard all of his stories. He sold what little we had after mom died, don't you remember? He sold the store, he sold my

---

grandfather's homestead, he rented an apartment in town so he could hold odd and end jobs, and be worthless for the rest of his dreary days. Over the last 15 years, I couldn't tell if he was drunk, or just completely out of it. Neither mattered, he always said what he wanted, and did as he pleased, with no disregard for me anyhow."

"Edmund Ross, he highly regarded you. He did everything in his power to keep you from his past. Please don't open this until we get back from court, please. We need to head that way. When we get back we will open his will. It's just a short walk, and the judge has set up a special time for us with a closed courtroom."

Jackson pushed back from his desk, and headed for his coat, hanging by his door.

"I need for you to be ahead of me when we leave. When we get to the courthouse we are going to Judge Tomlin's chambers. It'll just be him and the transcriptionist. His chambers are on the left corridor when you walk in the main entrance, 5th room on the right. Got it?"

Edmund nodded, confused why he wasn't walking in with Jackson. Jackson loaded what Edmund suspected was his father's registry and will into his briefcase, and gave final instructions to Edmund . "Put this letter in your coat pocket. Keep it there until we are done; then, we'll talk. Fifth room, left corridor. I'll be right behind you."

It was early on the morning of December 13th, 2015. A cold front was breaking over the Nantahala National Forest in the distance, and fog was crying over the ridge, as if mourning the death of one of it's own, one last time. He walked briskly out of the law firm, and crossed the street into the final hustle and bustle of the Christmas rush in downtown Hayesville. This rush was nothing compared to Raleigh. He only had to wait for one car before he could make it across the street. He climbed the courthouse steps, and pulled on the door. It creaked and echoed through the abandoned hallways and slammed shut with a loud boom. Every step he took echoed. He tried to walk faster, then slower, and finally settled on his normal gate. The echo reminded him of the last several years with his dad. Someone was there; he just wasn't sure who it was.

Chapter Three

The Fifth Room

The fifth room to the right wasn't hard to find. Judge Tomlin sat reading his paper, and his transcriptionist sat in silence waiting for the court record to begin.

Promptly at 8:45 a.m., Jackson walked into the room whispering to Edmund, "Not a word, best not guilty attorney face you can muster. Do not move a muscle." He understood those instructions as he'd heard that from Lisa on several occasions.

Honorable J. Tomlin

Tomlin cleared his throat, and his transcriptionist understood it was time for her to start keying.

"Records," Tomlin asked?

Jackson removed the red bound book and envelope from his bag. For several minutes all that could be heard was the turning of dried yellowed pages. The judge reviewed every entry for 15 years of records.

"Today, we close the estate of Porter Monroe Wise," Tomlin began. "The estate has satisfied the final wishes of the deceased, including one year of probate, and fulfillment of power of attorney by Attorney in Fact Stanley Albert Jackson. I have reviewed all records and in accordance with his final wishes, all properties, monies, physical property is now released to his son, and living beneficiary, Edmund Ross Wise. Mr. Wise, on behalf of Clay County, North Carolina, we extend our deepest sympathies to you over the loss of your father. He was a great man to this county just as his father was before him."

Edmund sat trying to process all of this as stoic as he could be. 'No emotion' he reminded himself as a single tear rolled down his cheek.

The judge continued, "Land deeds will be transferred effective today. The estate of Porter Monroe Wise will now be closed and placed in an individual account, divided between a trust and living expense account. Personal properties can be found in a storage container and are now your property. Mr. Jackson, I relieve you of your duties as Attorney In Fact for the estate of Porter Monroe Wise since his probate and final wishes have been carried out. The court thanks you for your service."

With that, the transcriptionist finished typing, picked up her stenotype, and quickly exited the room.

"Wise, this is yours. You deserve every penny that is there for all your father did for this county. Please find the exact records for your father's estate. After a careful and thorough examination, you'll find your remaining balance of 1.7 million dollars. The payment for the taxes will be processed today."

"1.7 Million dollars", Edmund said in shock. "Yes, after taxes. It'll be divided into two accounts, one for your daily use, and one for your future estate needs. You can go by the bank and pick up your new registry and checkbooks. They are expecting you."

"Land? What Land? He sold everything," Edmund said in shock and confusion.

Tomlin and Jackson looked at each other in disbelief. Edmund instantly knew they were both in on whatever all of this meant.

Edmund was more confused and angry than he was before. Why would his father live such a meek and lowly life, have all of this money and not touch it? Why would he not tell him about land? Whose land was it?

Tomlin and Jackson quickly decided that the courthouse was not the best place to continue this. Tomlin was concerned that his office was bugged, and that someone may be able to find out more than he wanted to share.

"Your truck or mine?" Tomlin asked.

"You know it better than I do, you drive." Jackson shot back.

"Wait, Wait, wait! I'm not going..." Edmund began.

He felt a strong arm fiercely grab hold of his shoulder, and a whisper, "Not a word, remember?" Jackson not so gently reminded him.

Tomlin exited his chambers, and told his stenographer to reschedule his cases until after the first of the year, that the three of them had decided to go hunting before the season closed. It was the one thing he was able to do as a judge; no one would complain.

They loaded up into a beat up old Chevrolet pick up truck. Jackson smarted off to Tomlin about how this wasn't his Mercedes. Tomlin knew, after the official meeting, there was going to be a private one. His hunting truck was the perfect cover.

As they were settling in the truck, the judge held out his hand, "phones" he demanded. Edmund and Jackson handed them over. He shoved them in the glove box and slammed it shut.

"Do we need directions?" Edmund asked from the back seat. The two old men laughed from the front bench seat, as the engine revved towards US 64.

"Son, go ahead, open that letter." Tomlin said.

He pulled it out of his right coat pocket, holding the envelope, faded, and yellowing. Written with ink from years ago, the letters were faded, but were still legible.

For: Edmund   R. Wise

He flipped the envelope over as they neared the stop light heading out of town. The envelope was sealed in one small spot, just as his father had always done, so he had no doubt on its authenticity. Tomlin and Jackson nervously sat and watched him from the front of the cab.

"Well, read the thing already." Jackson huffed.

"Outloud?" Edmund questioned.

"YES." he heard in unison.

Son,
Today you turn 19. You are somewhere in this world, though you don't call or write, so I'm not sure where.

You will not be pleased with how the next few lines of this will go, but I promise it's for the best.

Since 1942, I have lived a lie. My best friend, Stan Jackson and I have lived it together. For one year after my death, he will be my Attorney. He will manage all of my affairs. If he passes before me, I will do the same for his family.

Together, we have protected the heritage of Clay County, and until the first one of us passes, we will hold each other in confidence. After I am gone, and my estate is settled, you will inherit a large sum of money. I'm not sure how much it will grow to, but right now it's about $250,000.

I promise the money is legal, but when I accepted my portion, the deal was, it was only meant for those I left behind, and not for me to use unless I am unable to care for myself. My decision was made for me. Jackson will handle things for me, if I am unable to take care of myself. I am to do the same for him. That was part of the deal.

Trust only Jackson, and whichever Tomlin judge helps. I'm sure one of them will still be in power by the time you read this.

You will never know the real story, until long after I am gone. I never ran moonshine. It was never about running from the law. It's always been about Anna.

6-30-1999

P. M. Wise

One thing overwhelmed Edmund 's thoughts, Who was Anna?

Chapter Four

January 9, 1920

In the valley of the Nantahala Forest, a small cry was heard on a two hundred acre farm. It's a girl! It's a girl! I have a baby girl!

Layton Monroe Wise called out on his covered porch to his neighbor. James Jackson took off his hat and waved it back congratulating him on the new addition.

Anna Lizabeth Wise, as an infant
Anna Lizabeth Wise was the third of four children born to the Wise homestead. Her pale brown hair and sapphire blue eyes lit up the house filled with boys. She was the

only daughter of Lizabeth and Layton. She was the apple of their eye and gem of the valley. By 1930, the last of the children was born. One more "surprise": Porter Monroe completed the Wise household.

Inside the General Store

Layton ran the general store, which was the place to be in the 1930's. Farmers from around the valley would provide requests and receive shipments for all of their farming needs at Layton's store. Layton's was situated on the banks of the Hiawasee River, close to the Georgia/ North Carolina line. Lizabeth stocked the shelves and kept the floor swept while the children would run deliveries. This was usually between two farms namely The Jacksons and The Tomlins.

The three families were staples in the community. If you needed something it was usually from one of the three families. The Wise's ran the general store. The Jackson's patriarch was the attorney for the county, and the Tomlin family was the most prestigious- The county jail was tucked into his section of the valley.

John Tomlin managed to be judge and jury for all of the arguments that happened in the valley. This, of course, led to many many arguments between the Jackson's and the Tomlins.

Layton would invite the two men over for a 'sensible' meeting, on neutral ground, at the general store. Thankfully, it hadn't happened on too many occasions. But it had happened.

In 1931 devastation occurred in the valley. An outbreak of the flu spread in the wet cold winter. Some homesteads were hit harder than others. All three of the valley's high profile families lost members. The Tomlins lost two of their four children, the Jacksons lost one of their two. The Wise family was hit the hardest. Lizabeth and her two oldest children succumbed to the flu leaving Layton with Anna and Porter.

It was all he had: the store, the farm, and the two kids who looked just like their mother.

****

The funerals were held within days of each other. The graveyard grew in size in what seemed like overnight.

When the lot was full, Layton gave some of his land to keep everyone together. They held their breath after Lizabeth was buried. She was the last to be taken by flu in the valley.

The spring of 1932 brought the valley together. Some moved on, but three families stayed.

Chapter Five

The Gate

Jackson and Tomlin sat in the front seat motionless as if they had seen a ghost. As Edmund read the letter, he could hear sniffles from the front seat, and was certain he saw a tear running down Jackson's cheek. By this point they were rounding the outskirts of Lake Chatuge. The lake weaved in and out of the valleys as if it held the mountains together like glue.

"Ok, where are we going? My dad obviously trusted only your families. I'm not sure I trust anything at this point," Edmund said quite nervously from the back seat.

"We are hanging a left in just a minute. The first thing you need to see is your father's belongings. I've had them at my house for near close to twenty years. It won't take but a second. I'll be right back." Jackson came to a screeching halt as they pulled in his driveway. He slammed the old truck door shut and took off like lightning into the house.

"I sure hope he changes," Tomlin said.

Five minutes or so later, out he came in his hunting gear with two things: a small wooden box and a second pair of shoes.

He opened the back door to the truck, and handed both to Edmund. "You won't get answers in those loafers, I hope they aren't too big."

Edmund quite nervously set the box beside him to change his shoes. He was surprised at how small the box really was. It was only a little less than two feet long by a foot wide, and maybe six or seven inches deep. Hand carved and scraped, he ran his fingers over the top of the box, smooth and soft as velvet. He recognized it as the box his dad said was his grandfathers. Jackson said, "His life is in that box. It isn't much physically, but it's all of his memories. He lived through the contents of that box," Jackson told Edmund.

As if he was ready to step back in time, Tomlin reared up with excitement, rubbed his hands together and asked, "Alright, Edmund Porter, how much do you know before we get started with your history lesson?"

Edmund thought back to the mindless conversations he had with his father. Now he questioned everything in his mind as what was truth and what was fiction. Edmund began, "I thought he ran moonshine. I thought he was running from the law. He was always at court and was always in trouble it seemed. Other than that, I'm not sure what kind of history you are talking about."

Jackson shifted down into a lower gear. Wherever they were the pavement ended right beside the state sign that said "DEAD END", but the truck didn't stop. He kept on moving it forward down a well-worn path that paralleled the mountain to his left.

Tomlin said, "Son, we're talking about our heritage. How much do you know about Clay County?"

Edmund leaned back and said "Oh. I remember a little from my freshman year of high school. The TVA came in about 1941, and made Lake Chatuge so they could generate power for the valley."

"That isn't exactly as they presented it to us," Jackson said. "It was all about the war. We were entering WWII, and the TVA made it seem that if we did Lake Chatuge, we would be able to supply more power to help make more planes so our boys could come home. They knew we wanted our boys home from Europe. Most families would do whatever it took to get them back, even giving up their own livelihood, and farms, for the potential of bringing them home. Both of us had older brothers, and cousins who went to war, only a handful of them came back," Jackson remembered.

"We trusted them, we shouldn't have! None of us would be in all this mess if we had stood our ground." Tomlin smarted off, in a southern gentleman way.

"They would have just filled it up like they did with us there, or without us there," Jackson reminded him.

Edmund asked, "Wait, you didn't sell to the TVA? They claimed eminent domain?"

"Neither," Tomlin said. "They came in, said they were paying fair price, but that isn't what happened. After they gave us a deadline of December 31, 1941, they started clearing stuff themselves. By the 9th of January 1942, barns were on fire, houses were being destroyed, and those hooligans that moved in and took over were acting just like the Red Coats. Doing as they wanted, where they wanted, with no regard for anything or anyone."

Edmund felt his paralegal skills coming into play. He posed his question, already knowing the answer, "What happened on January 9, 1942?"

Tomlin shifted gears again, the RPM's revved as if to ignore the question. For the next 40 minutes Edmund sat in tension filled silence as they circled up and down the mountains of Western North Carolina.

Edmund opened the box to break the silence. On the top was a well worn journal. The cover was burned, but there were still some pages intact.

****

January 2, 1942

I've been in Hayesville for almost three months. I'd found a place to stay, and skillfully placed myself where I could fit in. It's my job to make sure I knew where every building, every fence, every human was.

I started with the Tennessee Valley Authority almost six months ago. They had needed me to keep track of the people, but they quickly realized I was much better at buildings, and objects, than I was with people.

This Hayesville General Store has just been emptied, much to the owner's refusal. All of it's contents were out a day or so ago, and my boss man took it over as his new space. For the next eight days, I'll be making sure everything is where it should be. Especially on the 10th. That's when we'll start removing all the structures, and clearing the way for the largest dam I've worked on.

I've got just one more section to map out. The owner has been less than helpful. He reminded me this morning, he was willing to give up the store, but his life depended on his land. It was all he had. I hope he knows it's nothing about him- It's what they sent us here to do.

I've struggled with this, it's the hardest part of the job. I've got money in my pocket, though. The TVA will pay them fair for their land, They can move into the mountains, just as those before them did. He'll see, it's for the best. Progress must move forward, and sometimes you have to sacrifice for the greater good.

I do like this town. This one is different.

January 3, 1942

This shop owner's daughter is a pistol. She came in here, stood toe to toe with the boss man, and let him know they better not set foot near that graveyard. Her heartbroken Pappy was weeping over the thought of having to move all 54 graves. She wanted to see the map, where the waters would be, how much time would they have. Were 'we' going to move the bodies.

Boss laughed at her, "They are dead girl! They don't matter! You best get your pappy out of here so we can move progress on along to this sleepy town." Then, she spat in his face! I've never seen someone so mad! He hauled off and hit her, it knocked her out cold! I told him that was enough, I got a cold rag for her face and helped her back to her feet. Her blue eyes pierced right to my soul. I've never seen such betrayal in the eyes of a woman. "My mamma is buried there with my brothers, you'll send my papa to an early grave too, if you don't stop!" She told him. "Some gave it all, your check is coming, just be thankful for what's coming." Boss stood his ground, and she slammed the door as she turned to leave.

****

"We're here," Tomlin said. Edmund sat the book back in the box and followed the men to the gate.

"Authorized Personnel Only. All Others will be prosecuted"

Edmund looked on as the two old men pulled out their keys, two locks, two different keys. Then they turned to Edmund , "Get yours! We need your key!" Jackson shouted. "In the box Jackass! Get your KEY!" Tomlin chimed in.

He ran back to the truck, opened the box, riffled through its belongings and there it was at the bottom: a locket with a single key on an old silver chain.

There Edmund stood, at the gate with two men he knew nothing about, all three turning their own lock at the same time. With that, the three locks popped in unison, the chain fell, and a loud groan came from the hinge as the gate swung open for the first time in nearly twenty years.

Jackson asked Tomlin about moving the truck. Tomlin answered, "I'll hide it where I usually do. I'd prefer for no tracks to turn in at the gates." Jackson agreed.

While Tomlin was moving the truck, Edmund asked why they would come up here if they didn't have the third key? Jackson laughed, "He's the moonshiner. His hiding drop off spot is just up the road. He's here at least twice a week."

"Figures" Edmund said, it would be the judge.

"I'm going to assume this is my property; the one you spoke of in your chambers." Edmund asked Tomlin.

"You sir, you are correct." he answered. "This is the property I spoke of. The one that has been held in trust, and hasn't been explored for near seventy years other than one time twenty years ago when we had to replace the locks. The three of us locked this place up in 1945. Your dad was the youngest. He was 15." Tomlin answered.

"Too young for what we did." Jackson mumbled.
"We were all too young" Tomlin said.

They clipped and stomped briars for what seemed like a half an hour, but it had only been ten minutes or so. The trees formed an arch that held the ancient gate and the secrets behind it.

The Smoky Mountains were living up to their names, and the fog could be seen in pockets coming out from the edge of the mountains. The sun was breaking through, and a stream could be faintly heard running over pebbles in the distance.

The path was small, and grown over. The mountain Laurel was thick from the years of overgrowth

"Welcome home," Jackson said
Edmund turned, to see Jackson patting Tomlin on the back.

"Thanks, I guess," Tomlin said.

"Wait, what?" Edmund asked.

"This was the old Tomlin Homestead, Your dad purchased this Edmund Ross, but it's still always gonna be home to me." Tomlin said.

In the valley Edmund saw what he now knew was a twisted family history of a homestead, but it was now his. Barely standing was a small house with a covered porch held up by four by four posts. There were no trees to be seen in the valley, but it was very marshy. To the left of the main house was a small shed on top of a stone foundation. Edmund thought to himself that neither looked safe, especially not the shed.

Jackson shuffled his feet and kicked the dirt underneath his shoes. He lifted his head from the memories this place brought back, and asked "Ready?" as if he knew that there was no turning back now.

Tomlin took one long last breath of freedom, and said "Yep", as the three of them started towards the house.

Edmund, being the city slicker he was, quickly said "Um, I'm not sure that's safe."

The friends laughed, and Jackson said, "It wasn't safe in '45! We know it isn't safe!"

"We'll be careful. Just watch your step," Tomlin directed.

They approached the house; the porch was falling off and the roof looked as if it was about to collapse. They moved on around to the back to a small set of stairs. Tomlin turned around to Edmund, and said "Follow me," and he disappeared into the homestead.

From the outside it was falling apart, but on the inside the house was still in order. The living room was set, photos still on the leaning walls, dishes in the cabinets, even glass on the bedside table. It was just as it was in 1945; the last time anyone was there.

As the floors creaked Tomlin gingerly meandered through the house. He moved through the house by memory knowing exactly what he was looking for.

"Here it is! I found it!" He heard Tomlin calling from the bedroom. "It's right where my dad left it. Under my granddaddy's pillow."

He slowly made his way into the doorway entrance with a glass flask. It was dark in color, and given their family history with moonshine, no one would suspect it.

"Come on! We're done in here! Let's get out before it falls!" Tomlin yelled. They both ran out to meet Jackson in the yard. The two old friends were laughing to the point of tears.

"What?" Edmund asked.

"You! That's what! You fell for it just like your father did! That board has been creaking since this place has been built. Your dad shrieked, and he had that same look the first time we pulled this on him, too!" Jackson was wiping the tears from his eye, and recomposing himself.

It was as if the three of them were teenagers playing tricks on each other.

As they stood in the yard Tomlin shook the bottle, and gave a nod in the direction of the shed, as if to direct his pals without saying a word. Tomlin led the way and started toward the old shed. He walked around to the bottom of the man made stone foundation. He took the bottle and with a firm grasp slammed it into the cornerstone. Glass shattered everywhere and a 'tink tink' could be heard on the ground.

"And I bet that key goes to another door," Edmund said.

"Well, something like that. Come on, follow me," Tomlin said.

Jackson hung back and kept watch as if he was still in his late teens being the look out.

"Edmund, this is where things get a little hairy. Maybe we should talk before we go further." Tomlin stopped and placed the key in his pocket. "Jackson, go get that box."

Tomlin walked with Edmund back to the rear of the house, and took a seat on the stoop. "It's going to take a few minutes for him, so here it goes... Your dad helped my family out of a big mess. We owed your grandaddy a lot of money. Your granddaddy and my grandaddy quietly made a deal with us to keep our reputation in tact for this piece of land. If he knew what the three of us did here on this land it would have killed him. I knew that your dad would end up with this land and Porter was a push over. He'd agree to anything. We were the only older brothers he had after all those folks got sick and died. He trusted us." Tomlin paused just as Jackson was rounding the corner with the box.

"That sure was a lot shorter walk twenty years ago." Jackson said.

"You were a lot younger twenty years ago." Tomlin said.

Edmund now had a better understanding of why his father joked the way he did. He got it from these two.

The box contained several photos, some of faces he knew, others he did not. There were a few postcards, the journal, and a few paper clippings about the TVA and a few other odds and ends in the bottom of the box.

"This is what your father lived with, what we hid and covered up. Anna knew what she was up to, and what she was up against. She had no fear and had us as her puppies. We'd follow her and do whatever she said. She was the one everyone swooned over. We all did," Jackson said to Edmund.

"Why didn't he ever talk about her? Why is today the only time I've ever heard her name?" Edmund asked. "Your dad made it easy- everything except for this photo was destroyed by the TVA. With nothing to prove she existed to him, she didn't." Tomlin said.

"Alright, light's almost up. We need to head back to town and come back in the morning. I don't need my truck lights back here after dark. I don't need that jackass of a sheriff seeing my truck back here. My cover'd be blown for sure." Tomlin said.

"Well, what am I going to do now? Edmund asked.

"I'd say dinner and a great bottle of wine! There's a great place downtown. You can't miss it. It's that new place with the copper doors; best steak around I hear," Jackson told him.

"Why the rush to spend my money?" Edmund asked.
"No rush, I just figured you'd like a nice meal. That's all," Jackson replied.

"It will have to be tomorrow; we didn't stop at the bank," Edmund said with a smug look.

For the next hour the three men discussed landmarks to help Edmund figure out where he was, and the upcoming plans for the new jail. They'd lived in the past too long today. It was nice to talk about the future.

Lake Chatuge was lit up with the reflection of the homes that filled its banks as they got closer to Hayesville.

"That lake holds a lot of our history," Tomlin said.

"Is that what happened to Anna?" Edmund asked.

"Why don't you look through the stuff in the box tonight, and we can fill in some blanks tomorrow on our way back to your new home." Jackson said.

The three men arrived back at the courthouse a little after seven. Edmund decided that a call to Lisa was in order so he could see what she thought.

He drove down by the high school, and sat in the parking lot. The view was but a halo of the moon's reflection on the tops of the mountains, but it was beautiful.

As the phone rang, Lisa answered. She sounded busy to Edmund.

She was speaking very softly. "Hello," he heard her say.

"Lisa, How do you hide 1.7 million dollars so no one knows?" Edmund asked quite nervously.

Lisa said, "You don't."

Edmund asked Lisa if she could talk, but she wasn't clear with her response.

"I'm at a meeting with Elaine. Your answer isn't justified," Lisa barked from the other end of the line.

Elaine was their code word. Lisa hated Elaine as much as anyone did. For her name to come up in conversation meant she was at social event and she was ready to go.

"Can you give me a few minutes? I will return your call. I am just a few minutes from being able to talk with you," she said.

Lisa never talked like that so he knew she was desperate to leave.

"Sure, I'll wait," Edmund said.

Five minutes went by without a single car passing.

"This is really a small town," Edmund thought.

He knew that there were other places to go, but this seemed like the most desolate place, and he hoped the view and talking with Lisa would help. The temperature was really beginning to drop. He hoped Lisa would hurry.

He didn't wait much longer before his phone rang.

"I'm sorry, I think I heard you wrong, Did you say, $1.7 million dollars?" Lisa asked astonishedly.

"Yes, that's what I said, and I have a piece of property,." Edmund replied quite frankly.

"What?" Lisa asked knowing the conditions his father lived in.

Edmund answered, "Lisa, This is really weird. The attorney and the judge know what is going on, but I am at a loss. They took me to a parcel of land that hadn't been opened in seventy years. They gave me a box that has some photos, a burnt journal from someone from the TVA, postcards, and a few trinkets, but that's it. That's all the physical property I have of my dad's. Then, here's where it gets odd. My dad had a sister. He never mentioned her. She's connected to all of this. They just haven't told me yet how everything is connected. And they are in on it too. The two of them are scared to talk. I've never seen anything like it. I mean, I know we have some quacks for clients, but nothing as crooked as a judge and the attorney in town hiding million dollar secrets."

Lisa said, "Edmund, use your best sleuthing skills. This isn't a divorce where we've found a cheating spouse, but you need to treat it as such. Start your timeline, and fill in what you know. If you know critical dates, write them down. You don't need to miss dates. There's more here to what they are telling you. I can taste it."

Edmund sat in silence for a few seconds just trying to process everything that Lisa had said. He knew she was right.

"Lisa, am I safe?" Edmund asked.

"Did your father leave you any messages?" she asked.

"Yes, to trust whichever Tomlin was in power, and Jackson." he replied.

"Then you should be fine. If you get to the point where you don't feel safe, call. You have your gun, right?" She asked.

His gun, he thought. "Yes, it's in the glovebox. I'll wear it tomorrow."

"You should have worn it today", she said.

"Listen, I'm going to Asheville after the Sampson case tomorrow. I'll be just a few hours from you. If I need to come over, let me know."

Edmund just wanted to hear her calmness in the situation. "I'll be fine. It's just a lot all at once. I had no idea any of this was as crazy as it is. I'm heading back to Leola's. I'll be heading back to my land with the two old farts who run this town first thing in the morning," Edmund said, trying to hide his anxiety.

"Edmund , do you know where your land is?" Lisa asked.

"Nope. I do know it's somewhere past Cold Branch, and well, past some place called Tush-quitti, I think."

"Well ok then. If something happens that confirms I'll never find you," Lisa smirked.

They both had an awkward laugh and said goodnight.

Edmund made it back to Leola's around 8. He was sure he had missed dinner, but he hoped she would have saved him some leftovers. He grabbed his box, the only clues he had to all of this, and headed in the old house.

The smell of lasagna beckoned him to the kitchen. "You look like you've seen a ghost! Come, sit, Eat child!" Leola said.

"I'm famished," Edmund said.

"And the ghost?" Leola pryed.

The wooden box sat next to him at the kitchen table.

He knew that she knew.

Chapter Six

The Other Guest

"Leola, I'm not ready to share. I've trusted you for many years. If I can't continue to trust you, I'll leave. I'm not certain of anything at this point, and I need a few more days to figure out what is going on. I don't need this whole podunk town in my business. I have a box and there are items in it. Right now, that's all I know." Edmund said aggressively.

"Hold your horses, sunshine." Leola barked back. "I know your family has lots of history in this town. I was just commenting on your facial expression. You look like you've seen a ghost."

"Not really a ghost. I'm just not sure what to make of things," Edmund said as he shoveled another spoonful in. "Hey listen, when was the last time you had a night out?"

"Not in a long, long time. I've just taken care of people so much it's my normal thing," Leola replied.

"Okay, tomorrow night dinners on me. Unless you've got another guest to take care of?"

Hesitantly, she answered, "Tomorrow, there will be another guest, but she's always quiet. Dinner sounds great. Is there room for three? But who is going to cook?"

"I heard there's a new place in town, We'll let them do the cooking. It's my Christmas present to you. I think I can afford a third wheel. Do you think he will mind?

"She," Leola began, " won't mind. Her name is Betty and she's as intriguing as they come." She said this with a giggle.

"Great, a gold digger, and I haven't even been to the bank." Edmund shook his head in shame.

"I don't think so, she's been here as often as you have just never at the same time. I'm truly surprised your paths haven't crossed before now. She stays here because she likes my cooking, and because it's quiet. She's an artist, humble and meek. She probably won't have a single word to say the entire meal," Leola said reassuringly.

"Well, that is a relief." Edmund said. He seemed to relax just a little, back into his comfortable relationship with his favorite innkeeper.

"Now Edmund, I'm honored you would even ask. And it will be nice to have a break from the kitchen for one night while I have company. Now, where did you find that box? I'd love to have something like that." She reached across the table to touch the fine craftsmanship.

"I think it's a one of a kind. My granddad made it if I remember,"

"I hope you find whatever it is you are looking for Edmund . I'm turning in. This old gal needs her beauty sleep. She's got a hot date tomorrow night!" She said this with a little spunk, and a sassy smile.

"He better treat my Clay County mama right!" Edmund replied.

"I'm sure he will" Edmund heard as she started down the hallway to her room.

Edmund thought back -- as long as he could remember he was certain Leola was a widow. In smalltown USA there wasn't a huge dating scene. She had always taken care of him, and treated him like her own. It was time for him to repay the favor. He'd rest easy tonight knowing the first person he'd spend money on was the person who has taken the best care of him through all of this, and an artist that she had taken a shine to.

He finished his plate, put his dishes in the dishwasher, and headed to bed.

The sunrise woke him before the alarm went off. The mountain sunrise was his favorite part of the room he always stayed in. The sky lit up with a faint blue before the pinks and oranges of the first rays of sun began to dance across the mountaintops. The sunrise over the mountains was one of the things he looked forward to the most. As he watched the sun start to rise in the east his brain started to think about all the things he had to do today.

How ironic, he was heading to the bank, and he would transfer a large sum of cash into his own name. His account had little to nothing in it depending on the day of the week back in Raleigh. He'd never have to worry with that again. The bank opened at nine so he had a few minutes to himself.

He was to meet up with Jackson and Tomlin at 10 so they could continue on their journey for answers. He wanted to be prepared with questions as best he could. He also wanted to look through the things in the box. Now was just as good a time as ever. He pulled it from the nightstand, and set it in front of him.

'Dad, if you are telling me something you need to show me what I need. I'm really lost.' He said this aloud to the ghost of a man long gone.

The hinge creaked as he opened it. He laid out it's contents: 2 post cards, 3 TVA news clippings, a burnt journal, locket, a handful of photos, a keyring filled with keys, and the key to the gate.

The TVA clippings were all information that was now found on the internet. The TVA offered $50.00 per acre for land. One showed some of the families on January 8, 1942, the day before the TVA destroyed everything. The other article talked about the graveyard in the middle of the lake. That one caught his attention more than others. It talked about how some of the bodies were moved, but that not all of them could be moved because of the time needed to exhume the bodies. The fact that the TVA was unwilling to give time for that to happen.

Anna, he knew, was in on that. 'That's why Dad had kept this article.' Edmund thought.

The two postcards were interesting. One had "I wish you would come to Hayesville" on the front. The other was a Christmas postcard from what appeared to be a family friend.

The postcard from Hayesville was odd he thought. Who would want to come to Hayesville? As he flipped it over his emotions charged as he saw who signed it: Anna.

I wish you would do what this postcard says. Come see me. Rescue me from this sleepy town.

Always,
Anna

The postmark was dated December 29, 1941. It was addressed to J. Faulk Route 4, Asheville NC. "
Anna had a secret love. But why did my dad have this postcard?"

The other postcard said:

Merry Christmas! It will be a few more days before we get Anna. We will get her on the 10th, so come after that. We will talk about what delayed her when we see you next week.

Rose & Tom Faulk

It was hard to read whom it was addressed to. It had been stored right beside the burnt journal and the words were smudged. Yet with Anna's being right next to it, he suspected it was J. Faulk's. "Great. Someone else I have to hunt down," Edmund thought.

Raymond, TVA Inspector

He sat those aside, and looked at the photos. One he recognized as his grandfather, wrinkled, but well defined in a nice suit. Another photo was much smaller. The photo was of a man in a tightly brimmed hat, similar to a postman's hat, in a suit. He wasn't dressed in military gear, and he knew it was a uniform he had never seen before. He'd have to ask who this was. The only name he could make out was Raymond. Hopefully this would be a duplicate person and not another puzzle piece he thought to himself.

Anna Lizabeth Wise

The last picture he picked up was Anna. Her name was written on the photo dated 1941. Sandy brown hair with high cheek bones. The picture may have been black and white, but he knew she was probably the most desired twenty something that lived in Hayesville.

She was very well put together. Her hair had waves and well-kept curls, and given the shades on her face she had blush on her cheeks. Her lips were just enough to tease anyone who walked by, and he imagined that she was just as feisty as her brother. All of that added up to be a handful in a dress. He smiled at the thought. Anna was a Wise, one of the most beautiful women he knew to be in his family tree. He'd found a lost part of his family.
He picked up the journal, and studied the burned exterior. It was black on the edges, but mostly together on the binding, and interior pages. He carefully opened the pages to continue reading.

Jan. 4, 1942

Talked with landowners about gravesite. New property has been located to move 15 of the graves. Moving the bodies will begin in the morning, as long as this storm moves on. We expect that not all of the graves will have to be moved, some will be above the water table level, we will not move the ones that are above water level. It's cold and snowing today. Bossman said it should clear tonight. We will have to work twice as hard if it doesn't clear to keep us on schedule.

Jan. 5, 1942

Snow.

Jan. 6, 1942

The snow is lighter today, about 6 inches of accumulation. Locals are moving last things out of the flooding zone. Wise's have made progress; they seem to be the lone holdout. The daughter has started moving things through the snow, but not as much as others.

Jan. 7, 1942

It stopped snowing in the night, and the temperature seems to be on the rise. I had made it as far as the Wise homestead today before I met trouble. The Wise clan was standing on the porch, guns in hand, refusing to move anything else, until we promised to move their family graves. I showed them on the map that their family plots would be above the flood stage, and would be on an island in the middle of the lake. Mr. Wise would have nothing of the sorts. When I heard him loading his rifle, I began to run. I fell in the snow when I heard the rifle discharge. Then I heard them laughing. Bossman said we would go talk with them tomorrow.

Jan. 8 1942

We delivered notice to the Wise Farm today with the Tomlin judge. We told Mr. Wise , that tomorrow we would start the deconstruction of the farm, by all means necessary. We informed him that we would be there promptly at 9 in the morning to tear things down. He loaded his shotgun again. My bossman pulled out his pistol and cocked it asking if he really wanted this to end in a gunfight. The judge was able to calm him, and started moving towards the porch. He lowered his weapon. He knows we will be back in the morning.

Edmund turned the page to see nothing. Not a single entry more. Whoever wrote this was part of the mystery.

An hour had passed while he looked through the memories. He jumped out of bed and ran to the shower. "Crap! I'm gonna be late!" he yelled at himself.

"IT'S A TWO MINUTE WALK! YOU WILL MAKE IT" He heard Leola scream up the stairs. Yep, he thought, she deserves a real good dinner.

Chapter Seven

The Hayesville Bank

As he headed over to the Hayesville Bank Tomlin was pulling into the street side parking. "Morning, Son! How is Leola today?" Tomlin asked.

"Just fine, I guess. I am taking her with me to dinner tonight. I don't think she's had a date in years, and it seems fitting to take her. I hate eating alone," Edmund replied.

Tomlin chuckled at the thought, and with a simple nod, Edmund knew he was making the right choice.
The old door creaked behind the weight of the glass as they entered the bank. The manager was waiting for them.

Nathaniel Clay Gibbs, Bank Manager

"Good morning Gentlemen. If you will follow me." Nathaniel Clay Gibbs, short in stature, but great in heart, had been expecting the youngest Wise for a very long time.

The manager quickly ushered them into his office. The tellers stood behind the counter eyes wide open. He knew they had just seen the richest man in the county.

As they sat in the office he could tell that it had just been updated to a modern bank. The glass door seemed to be the last thing that remained of the old bank. The chairs and desks were modern in style. It gave a higher-class feel to the old town.

"Mr. Wise, how would you like to make this withdrawal? by wire transfer?" Gibbs asked.
Edmund dropped his head and smiled. "This is just like my dad," he said sternly.
"And what do you mean by that, Sir?" Gibbs questioned out of fear.
"He always wanted me to come back here to live. I hated this place, and he knew the only reason I was coming was to close the estate. I was only supposed to gather his belongings and go home. I hadn't planned anything for the money because I knew there was none. He didn't tell me. There's no bank in Raleigh that I trust. I'd rather it stay here. It's too risky to move it until I know what I am doing, and figure this entire thing out. Can you just keep the funds here, please?"

Edmund made the inquiry with complete trust in the establishment that had taken great care of his father. "Absolutely, It's our pleasure to serve you just as we have done for your family for years," Gibbs replied.
Tomlin and Edmund looked at each other in agreement. They thought that it probably was the best thing for the time being until he had made decisions on what was going to happen. Mr. Gibbs needed just a few signatures and gave him a temporary checkbook.

Edmund shook his head. It didn't even have his name on it, and he had more money than he knew what to do with.

"I do have one request," Edmund started. "I'd like a little pocket cash. How much did my Dad carry?"
In unison Tomlin and the Gibbs said, "Ten thousand dollars".

"What! You let that old man carry that much money? Why did he need that much?" Edmund asked shockingly.
"Well," Tomlin said, as he scratched his forehead as if trying to figure out what to say, "He didn't need it. He never knew when he was going to see something he wanted, or see someone who needed something. I promise, it was more of the second than the first. When his dementia started up, he came to my office one day in tears. He never said who, but someone figured out how much money he was carrying. That was the last day he carried that much."
"That's when Jackson took over his finances. Right then," Edmund said.

"Right." Tomlin answered.

"Ten thousand it is," Edmund said as he completed his withdrawal slip.

Mr. Gibbs walked from the room and returned rather quickly bringing back a large envelope of bills.

"I'd hoped you would honor your father by withdrawing his special amount. I had it prepared in my vault just in case." the manager said.

"Thank you, Sir. I'm sorry, I didn't catch your name?" Edmund asked.

"Nathaniel. Nathaniel Clay Gibbs,." he said.

"Well, Mr. Gibbs, thanks for taking care of my dad."

"Edmund Wise?" Mr. Gibbs asked.

"Yes, sir?" Edmund replied.

"Have you figured out where the money came from?" Gibbs inquired.

"Nope," he replied sharply.

"Well then," Gibbs began, "wherever it came from it is an honor to serve your family."

****

"Well, are you ready to put some of this together, son?" Tomlin asked as the doors to the bank creaked shut.

"More than ever," Edmund said.

Tomlin pulled the key from his coat. Edmund could see that it was an old skeleton key, and was certain it was the key that was from the broken bottle. Tomlin could see that he was eyeing it.

"Go ahead," Tomlin said.

"What?" Edmund replied.

"Ask," Tomlin said.

"Fine. Where does that go?" Edmund smarted back to him.

"Just for that doggone attitude I ain't tellin."

"Huh?" Edmund raised his eyebrow in confusion.

"I'll just have to show you. Do you need a blindfold today? Or are you actually going to try and learn where your land is?" Tomlin asked.

"I'd guess, I'd better learn. No time like the present," Edmund said.

"I was hoping you'd say that!" Tomlin threw him the keys to his beat up truck. Edmund, still in a bit of shock, caught them just before they hit the ground.

"You drive!" Tomlin shouted.

"Okay? So, back to Tush-quitt-ee?" Edmund asked, knowing he just butchered the name.

"Nope, Cold Branch," Tomlin said.

"Cold Branch? Where's Cold Branch? Why are we stopping there?" Edmund questioned.

"Well, if you must know, it's right past Peckerwood. We gotta pick up Jackson. Then, we can go towards Tusquitti," Tomlin replied.

"Peckerwood!" Edmund laughed hysterically as he cranked the truck. "I don't want to know the reason it's named that, do I?"

"Nope," Tomlin replied with a smirk on his face.
"I bet that is a popular street sign, huh?" Edmund jokingly asked.

"After it was stolen for the 25th time, they finally cemented the thing in the ground."

Edmund now knew his first landmark to his new 'home'- a cemented street sign.
Twenty minutes after leaving the square of Hayesville he passed the sign. A right, a left, and a right later they saw Jackson's house. Jackson was standing on his porch waiting for his ride.

As much as the two men tried to give vague descriptions of "left at the old pond" or "right just past the dead tree", Edmund still managed to miss two turns, and almost ran off the side of the mountain. He had never been as happy to see a dead end street sign.

This is where "off the grid" began. Thirty minutes later, the crisp winter morning greeted him at his gate.

Edmund was home.

Chapter Eight

January. 9, 1942

Jackson had a perfect record. He knew who was where and
if a theft occurred he had an arrest made. Every murder
was solved and he was proud of that. The TVA brought
thousands of workers that took his sleepy little town into a
transient party. The jail was full, and the local
'establishment' had roughnecks crawling home from the
nightly fill of intoxication. At times it seemed to be more
than his family could bare. The jail was on the second
floor of their home, and its tenants often made more
trouble than they were worth.

Tomlin had told him the evening before of the anger and
decision that Layton had made. He wasn't leaving his
home. Jackson wanted to make sure he knew what went
down so he met the TVA boss man and inspector at their
office,. This had previously been Layton's general store.

There would be no second-guessing if something happened. Over the last month several homes were moved or burned, and the Wise Farm was the sole holdout for the progress of the TVA.

"This is the last house in this section that has to go. I've confronted him, and I'm not certain what to do now. He goes or he's going with it," Raymond said.

"Raymond, if you can't do this, I'll do it. We've got to get them out of there. The dam is almost ready, and the waters will be released in a month. It's got to get done." the TVA Bossman said.

"Boss, it's my job so let's not jump to conclusions. He will move. They always have. I've done it before and I'll do it again. Sheriff, you ready?" Raymond asked hesitantly.

Jackson nodded and buttoned up his jacket. He hated to see all of this fertile land gone, but he valued his friendship with Wise. He knew for progress to continue in this sleepy little town the TVA had to get out of there as quickly as they came. Unfortunately, that meant that the last standing homestead, the Wise Farm, would have to be torn down.

Porter Wise, Tomlin, and Jackson were huddled at the barn where Layton had told them to go. Layton didn't want them to be involved. He told them, no matter what, not to move unless they were given specific instructions to do so. With one final hug, and a "go on, son", he sent them out of harm's way.

The car pulled up with the sheriff and the TVA employees. It was a cold crisp winter morning that would end in a blaze of fire.

****

"Do we have to keep putting three locks on this fence?" Edmund huffed.

"I guess that is up to you, but it is the backwoods, and you really don't have a clue about who is around here, so yes," Tomlin smarted back.

As much as Edmund thought it was ridiculous he knew it was the truth. There was easy access past the gate, and the multiple locks did seem to be a deterrent.

Tomlin and Jackson inspected the roadway for other tire tracks. Tomlin seemed to be assured that the hunters had not stopped or noticed any change in the plot or gate. He felt confident to continue on with the vehicle to it's hiding spot.

There wasn't a wasted minute on the ride to Edmund's property. He began to hear the stories of the TVA members coming in and the Inspector, Raymond, who had been confrontational with Layton Wise. Edmund learned that Anna had only sent word of her marriage just days after she changed her name to Mrs. Faulk. Her conversation, though brief, validated the events that she saw that day. When they asked if she would return the phone call was disconnected. No matter how many times the operator tried to reconnect the call it would never go through.

Tomlin and Jackson had been told of the details just to keep the story truthful even though it was silent. It was still history, and one that deserved to be recorded in the living memory of the few.

January 9th, 1942

Anna had packed her bag and hidden it near the old barn. Tonight she would run away to meet Jeffrey Faulk, her sweetheart. They were set to meet at the pass, and would continue on towards Asheville.
They were set to be married in Asheville on the 11th. She was finally through with this dreadful town, and it was fine with her if she never saw it again. She would be his wife before he left on Monday to enter WWII. His draft date was set, and being Jeffrey's wife was all she wanted.

PFC Jeffrey Faulk

Anna passed the boys as they were heading to the barn. She could hear the doors shutting on the old car, and could see smoke coming from the chimney. She picked up her pace, and hid just before the gate.

With her pistol at her side, she made sure her gun was ready if she had to protect herself. She was afraid of what her father would do.

After last night he had been talking out of his head, and she was scared.

Three men stood near the front porch. Layton stood in the doorway of his home, long arm rifle open and ready for ammunition.

"I'm not leaving!" She heard her father scream.

"Layton, come on! It's not worth it! Think about your boy and Anna. They need you!" Jackson said as he urged him to come off the porch.

"They are better off without me! I have nothing left!" Layton bantered back as he stepped closer to the door.

"Let's be civil; we are paying you good for your land. You can move your house. I'll have the men start today," Raymond said.

"You are paying me nothing! This is my land! I'll go with it!" Anna heard her father scream.

She knelt and covered her mouth with her shaking hands to keep from screaming. Tears were streaming down her face. As she cleared her eyes, she saw that her father had gone back into the house which was filling with smoke from the uncontrolled fire he had set inside, the smoke was no longer just coming from the chimney.

"Layton! Get out here!" Jackson screamed.

Just then, Layton appeared with a loaded gun still standing just inside the door.

"I'm not leaving! I'll kill you before you take my land," Layton said as he chambered his rounds.

Without hesitation Raymond pulled out his pistol and was at a dueling stance with Layton. Jackson and the Bossman had backed to the car for cover, and had drawn their weapons pleading with Layton to end this.

Layton urged Raymond, "You have to the count of three to get off my land! ONE!... TWO!...."

Two shots were fired.
Raymond laid motionless in the front yard.
Layton began to groan and turned back into the burning home.

Jackson tried to go in after him, but the flames were too hot. Layton stumbled out the back door without anyone noticing and died still holding his gun.

Chapter Nine

The Truth about History

Edmund sat motionless on the collapsing front porch. The stoic behavior of his possessed father now made perfect sense. He began to see the horror that his father witnessed at such a young age, and why he mysteriously reverted to a time he knew little about. Edmund knew that the age of his father and the timeline of his stories never added up.

Now, he understood why. Porter Wise had blocked years of his life and created a fantasy parallel lifeline that he could survive in.

Edmund clenched the box his grandfather had made, white knuckled out of fear. He had never felt such anguish. The grief his grandfather must have felt after creating a life, and watching it slowly be ripped to shreds. Leaving a once towering pillar of the community, as a man who took his last breath fighting for the small amount of the world that he called his own.

Edmund tried processed everything he was hearing. The journal entries, the write ups in the newspapers, the now seemingly fictional history lessons he was taught his entire life, of how peaceful the transition was for the Clay County citizens when the TVA rolled into town.

Clay County wasn't better because of the TVA. They were broken. The fertile lands were gone; washed under millions of gallons of water.

The joyous community and pride was beaten, dragged and burned right out of their hands. The people were forced to move to higher land where water wasn't as easy to find, and the soils were much more difficult to work with. The peaceful valley was gone, and now Edmund was beginning to understand the true story that changed Clay County history.

****

The 'Only' Fatality.

Jackson turned to see Bossman kneeling over Raymond's body. "He's the only man I've lost. How am I going to explain this?" Bossman asked.

"Very simply. He died trying to save Layton. I'm your witness. We will have him buried with little to no noise. There won't be enough of Layton to dispute anything," Jackson continued.

"You don't want trouble; I don't want trouble. We both saw what happened. It's going to be for the best. Let's make this look as if he is the hero. Everyone knows how defensive Layton was over his land. It will be believable." Jackson said.

Jackson was quick on his feet with his words trying to make sure he would get the best end of the deal out of the situation. The TVA had gotten enough of the good end of the stick.

"Right," Bossman said.

Just then, the three boys appeared trying to figure out what was going on.

Jackson told the Tomlin boy to go get his daddy.

Porter Wise stood screaming trying to figure out what was going on, and where his daddy was.

"Son, he ran back in. We couldn't stop him. The fire was too hot." Bossman said.

Porter Wise, as a child

Porter's sorrows filled the valley. Anna could hear him crying as she neared her bag. She turned to see the blaze and whispered, "good bye".

She continued on with her plan. By this time next week she would be married, and the wretched life of the valley would be but a memory.

Tomlin arrived to see Jackson and the Bossman kneeling over Raymond's lifeless body. Jackson gave Tomlin a rundown of how things played out, that Layton went back in and never came out. The judge sighed and threw his hat on the ground. He ran to the back of the house only to find Layton laying in the yard. He yelled, they came running; their simple plan was simple no more. Now they had one body to bury and one to hide.

Young Tomlin was consoling Porter when his father came running to him.

"Son, I'm going to need you to drive. Jackson, I'm going to need your help. Porter, I'm sorry son, but now we have to take care of you until we find Anna. Load up, we have to take a ride." The eldestTomlin without hesitation took over, like he had always done before.

Young Tomlin knew something wasn't right, but he was afraid to ask any questions. In unison, the three boys said yes sir, and followed instructions.

Porter and Young Tomlin were backing the truck to the fence as young Jackson and the Judge walked toward the back of the house.

"There are few things in life that happen that we never speak of. The truth will destroy us. We will fill in the gaps. You tell the other two they were with you. None of you can ever say a thing. You listen to us; we will get through this. Now we are moving a body. It got ugly, and we have to take care of this. Your daddy is handling the TVA. We have to handle Layton. I know where we will bury him, I just need you to get him there."

Young Jackson began to tear up as the judge gave him instructions to an old farm. The Judge reassured him that it would be hard, but they would survive.

Carefully, they wrapped Layton's body in a sheet of burlap from the barn, and carried him to the car. As carefully as they could, they laid his body in the trunk. His rifle laid beside his body. The boys sat in the front.

"Remember where I told you to go, the old homestead, right?" The judge asked young Jackson.

"Yes sir. We will wait for you," he replied.

"Take care of Porter. If you see Anna, pick her up. We will be there as soon as we can," the judge assured him.

It was nearly an hour's drive through the mud to the homestead. Porter whimpered in his sleep as the older boys formed their plan. The three of them would take care of each other, no matter what.

****

The cold chill of the crisp mountain air faded as Edmund's blood boiled. Tomlin and Jackson could see the anger beading in his eyes.

"Edmund Ross, let's walk," Tomlin said.

"Where. There's nothing here," Edmund snapped back.

"Alright, where would you like to start, you've got a couple of options within a few feet. What building would you like to explore?" Jackson asked.

"Well, we could start with that skeleton key and old shed," Edmund replied inquisitively.

"The old shed, huh? Well, I guess that would work," Tomlin said.

Tomlin tossed the key to Edmund, and gave him a look. Edmund was fairly certain this wasn't just a shed. This skeleton key, he thought, had to be around a hundred years old. The lock was just as geriatric as the key, but they fit together like a glove. The lock popped open and the door swung open with seventy years of secrets begging to escape.

"What is this?" Edmund said, as his voice echoed for what seemed to be a long distance.

He didn't need an answer, as the sunshine broke through the darkness, he saw an old cement cross leaning against a second entry way further down this skinny corridor.

The cross said one word.

"Mother"

Chapter Ten

The Cover Up

With the TVA now having a death on its hands the Bossman was beginning to panic.

"How am I going to explain this? What about that boy?" Bossman asked Jackson.

"We will bury Raymond in the Wise grave. We will tell the TVA boys the fire was so hot that there was nothing left, and that this is Wise, so our town can bury this without too many questions. This plan is going to cost you. You better be ready. You've gotta pay for that boy. Him and his sister got nothing now," Jackson said.

"Whatever it cost. Let's get this settled, and get this boy buried first," Bossman said.

"I don't think so," Jackson said. "Pay us first, you can call it a land or fruit bonus then we bury him. We'll take the body back with us, and I can get the coffin for his body."

The constant motion of new TVA employees made it easy for the story to be bought. They all knew the dangers of burning the buildings, and since he died a 'hero', trying to save Layton, the townspeople bought the story as well. A simple coffin was made, of pine panels and 'Layton' was buried by Lizabeth before the sun went down. Burnt flesh smelled they told the town. That's why he had to be buried so quickly.

In the cover of night, a judge and sheriff went to bury their best friend. With his son by their side, he was buried in the damp catacombs of an old abandoned corundum mine. Within a week, his deceased wife and children would be with him, each moved in the darkness of night. As the last body filled the catacomb, the final penance payment was made. Three separate payments of $25,000 were made. One for the land, one for Anna, and one for Porter.

The last building to be destroyed was the general store. The fire was set, and a crowd gathered to watch an era burn to the ground. The smoke was only starting to billow when Bossman realized his records were still inside. The

Tomlin boy rushed in, retrieved the stack of records, and saw the journal laying on the desk. Its cover was beginning to burn as he brushed off the flames and tucked it under his arm.

The crowd cheered when he jumped from the banded porch. He handed the papers over to Bossman Not recognizing the journal, he told the brave lad he could keep it. Filled with eight days of journal entries, and a single photo, young Tomlin had the only proof that Raymond ever existed.

****

Edmund's heart was in his throat, as he heard somber sobs behind him.

"Tell me. Tell me now," Edmund demanded.

"This is Clay County's biggest cover up. We moved them all in the dead of night. It's a smell I will never forget," Jackson began. "We dug out shelves in the soft corundum mine walls, and laid each casket in their own place. It's what your granddaddy would have wanted."

As they eased slowly back towards the second entrance, Edmund saw the shadows of dilapidated caskets just beyond the narrow opening.

"What else is back there?" Edmund questioned.

Tomlin replied, "Nothing. Absolutely nothing. We searched and searched for years and years in that hole for anything of value. Nothing ever turned up other than a few rubies and garnets."

"So, that is what my grandfather rescued your family from. Financial worry." Edmund realized.

With a nod, Tomlin walked by Edmund to place a soft touch on the decaying wooden coffins. The moisture was still low in the mine shaft which kept the decay to a minimum.

Edmund followed Tomlin further back in the mine to see two shelves that were empty. He knew those had to be for his father and for Anna. His father had been buried beside his mother in a cemetery clear on the other side of the lake.

Anna's empty spot left more questions than there were answers. All that could be seen were fragments of a multiple rose stems where her casket should have been, if she wasn't still alive.

****

January 11, 1942

As Hayesville is reeling from the aftermath from the prior days, Anna had made her way to he beau. She was overjoyed to be with his family, as she skirted questions of her family and why they were not able to join for the wedding, she told Jeffrey she was ready to be his bride. After the heartache she had endured, she didn't want to wait any longer. They made a plan to sneak away and marry that day, instead of a few days later at church. He didn't have much time left before he would be shipped off, and she wanted to spend every minute she could with him as his wife.

PFC J. Faulk, married Anna in Asheville on a snowy morning in front of the city judge. Her heart was content, her dreams sealed with a kiss, charged her with forever being the bride of PFC J. Faulk.

Chapter Eleven

Time Changes People

Edmund was beside himself. His emotions ranged from fear and anger to a small sense of comfort. He was satisfied knowing most of his family was together. He turned to Tomlin to ask how they were able to hide this for so long, but he realized it was just him standing in his family crypt.

He exited the mine with tears streaming down his face searching for the lock through a flood of tears. There was nothing left for him in this building. No reason for him to return to this. He had seen enough here. He found the lock lying on the ground, and quickly relocked the door. He turned to Tomlin and Jackson now understanding why he had no say in his father's wishes.

Jackson said, "My dad took him in; he was my brother. He was loved as a Jackson, but he obviously didn't handle it all well. He spent many years trying to block the days before the TVA released the flood waters. He could never fully tell you what was real and what wasn't. It was as if he had PTSD. He had moments where he had fits of rage. My mother would hold him and rock him until he fell asleep.

He faintly remembered this property for years near Lake Nantahala. He was about twenty before we really talked about it. He was so little when everything happened. He had been asking questions about the graveyard when my dad decided he needed to know. We loaded up in the truck, one spring day, and headed out here. That's when he started bringing the roses for Anna. He would come every year on her wedding anniversary and lay a single rose for her.

In the Seventies we brought him out here one last time, and begged him to lock it up. In hindsight we probably shouldn't have. It kept him sane, having a place to mourn, but he was dwelling in it more and more. It was becoming an obsession. He wanted justification, and he simply couldn't have it and continue to live a regular life. We took him out of state to see a psychiatrist to hypnotize him. We gave him a fake history. We gave him the storyline of the Tusquittee boys, and the moonshiners history. He came home thinking he was in full recovery from being an alcoholic, which was why his memories were fuzzy. He could only remember fragments, and only that his family was buried in a catacomb in the mountains.

My father paid the tax bill for years until he began to ask where the grave was. Thankfully, that year the waters were higher, it had rained a lot, and we honestly couldn't get back to the property. That's when we decided we needed to fill him in on what he had intentionally forgotten. You were little, your Ma wasn't sick yet, but he was desperate for information. He began to search through history records and court records trying to remember every detail."

"That is why I remember Mom fussing about him being at court all the time." Edmund said.

"Right," Jackson continued, " We couldn't keep him from the courthouse and the library. He wanted every detail so he could understand why history was written the way it was. It was hard for him to find more than what you currently see. I swear that the newspaper journalists were paid by the TVA to keep their stories positive. So that is how history was written, in a positive light, no matter what history truly looked like."

Tomlin stood stoic with his hands in his pockets shuffling his feet. He seemed like he had something to say, but wasn't sure how to say it.

"What? What do you want to say. NO Secrets!" Edmund yelled.

"This is where what we know ends. I can't explain the amount of money in your account. Your father only started that after you began to drift from his life. He wanted better for you. And he wouldn't tell us anything. There's more for you at the courthouse with the register of deeds, and you should probably talk to the town historian. The rest of these out buildings are full of random things from our lives. It's all yours. He blocked me out of his life, and blamed this cover up on me. I don't know why. I missed my friend, but I swear I have kept your family's secret," Tomlin said in shame.

"Fine. Can you get me back to Leola's? And, I would really appreciate a few days before I see the two of you again. I've got a lot to process and I just want to process some of this on my own," Edmund said in pain.

He needed to think on his own. He had so much to process, so much he didn't understand. He needed to talk to Lisa, but also knew, he had to gather his thoughts and recompose himself before dinner tonight. And that was going to take some time.

They walked to the gate, each of them locked their individual locks and loaded back into the pickup truck. This time, they gave the keys to Edmund. It was his now.

****

June 25, 1942

Anna was hanging clothes on the back line when she heard the dirt crunch in the driveway under the weight of a heavy

---

106

vehicle. She grabbed the last clothespin from her apron pocket to finish hanging her bed sheets when she heard the car door shut, twice. She began to shake as she heard two sets of footsteps approaching her house, their house.

She ran around the house to meet two Army Officers dressed in Class A uniforms. She fell to her knees as they turned to see her. She screamed before they could even say a word. She knew why they were there. There was only one reason. Her Jeffrey was gone.

She could hear them giving condolences above her uncontrollable sobbing, but could barely understand the words. She was supposed to have him home to live a long life. She didn't want to comprehend that he was gone.

Four days later, at an empty grave, her 'new' family held a funeral for PFC. J. Faulk.

Twenty One gunshots.
A single folded American Flag.
Anna's forever broken heart.

That's all Anna had left to hold onto of his memory.

****

Edmund had recomposed his thoughts by the time he was climbing the steps to Leola's. He had decided he would spend Christmas here, and unsure of what he was going to do, or how much time all of this would really take. He had decided he would contact Lisa to let her know he would need more than just a few days. It may be a few weeks; he just wasn't sure.

He was mumbling to himself as he walked in. He could hear the giddy humming of Leola as she was getting ready. He needed a shower and flew up the stairs to get himself together. As he topped the stairs, he was watching his feet to make sure he made the last step when he ran head first into Betty. She gave a squeal of surprise since she had her head buried in a book, looking downward.

"Hi," Betty said, as she skirted around him and down the stairs.

Betty Anne Cofield

Edmund watched as she gracefully walked down the stairs, head buried in her book without missing a step, and barely making a sound. He thought, 'Well, wasn't that an introduction?"

Betty turned around at the bottom of the stairs when she realized he was still standing at the top of the stairs gazing at her.

"I'll be ready by six and so will Leola, so don't be late," she said, with a slight blush to her cheek.

"I don't have far to go so I shouldn't be." Edmund said.

Her simple beauty struck him. Leola had conveniently left that out. He knew she was mild mannered and humble just by the appearance and grace he had just seen. He felt at ease, that his third wheel to Leola's date would be an intriguing addition in company. He hoped he just wouldn't be a bumbling mess every time he looked into her deep green eyes.

He took a deep breath, turned to his bedroom door, and got ready faster than he ever had. He suddenly didn't like any of the shirts or sweaters he had brought with him from Raleigh. He was standing in front of the mirror with one long sleeve button up shirt and one sweater. Swapping them back and forth trying to decide which one looked best on him. He was beginning to get frustrated when he heard a familiar giggle coming from behind him. He quickly turned to see Leola standing in the doorway, arms crossed and shaking her head.

"Pick the sweater. She'll like the sweater," Leola said.

"Thanks," Edmund said hesitantly.

"She won't bite and neither will I. Now, are you almost ready? I'm hungry, and for the first time in years, I won't be fixing my own supper," Leola replied with a smirk.

Edmund rolled his eyes with a half smile and a laugh. He shook his head as he put on the sweater. He tied his shoes and told her he was ready.

The Copper Door was really all it was made out to be. The atmosphere was elegant, and the wait staff was impeccable. The chef was world renowned, and to be in such a small town, it truly made the experience that much more enjoyable. As Edmund, Leola and Betty began their meal, it was all Edmund could do to keep from taking up all of the conversation. His nervousness from the butterflies he had felt at the top of the stairs, kept him chatty. He would try to ask questions about Betty, but Betty quickly turned the questions around to ask about the last few days and what he had learned about his history. She would quiz him on details, small things that a man would usually not remember and write them in her journal. She assured Edmund he could have the pages; it was just easier for her to write everything, than to try to remember.

"So, where are you going to start tomorrow? Betty asked.

"I've been asking myself that question all day," Edmund began, "I guess I need to find the library in this little town and start there. Hopefully they will have the documentation I need, and a map or something to tell me where are the vital records are kept."

Betty instantly stopped writing and began to look at Edmund with shock and distaste.

"What?" Edmund asked glaringly.

"You really have no clue where to start do you?You really don't have a single clue about this town," Betty said as she shook her head and continued on with her note taking.

"And you do?" Edmund asked firmly.

"Obviously more than you do, and I've never lived in this town," Betty smarted back.

Leola began to chuckle with her arms crossed at the two of them. Two opposite ends of the spectrum sitting at the same table she thought. She knew she had to take charge of this, or it would ruin the best dinner she had had in years.

"Now listen," Leola began, "Edmund get over yourself. You haven't been here in years, and you have little to no knowledge of how this town has changed in the last fifteen or so years. Lucky for you, Betty does! She is a history major, and has made Hayesville her little pet project for years. She spends more time in books, than she does painting. She knows where to find the historical documents, where the vital records are, and probably where to find what all those keys go to. And you aren't gonna start at the library, you'll start at the historical society, just the other side of the square. That's where all the information on Hayesville and the TVA is. That's where you'll find the best information, the best leads and all of the real articles on what happened when. Then, after your history lesson, you can take sweet Betty with you to the new courthouse where are all of the deeds are in that big ole building. You can go talk to the Register of Deeds office, and get everything put in your name. THEN, you can go to Jackson County and do the same thing for that dilapidated shed, and corundum mine, since that isn't in this county. Are we clear?"

He answered with the only thing he could muster up,

"Yes, Ma'am."

Betty's cheeks began to blush, Leola had just summed up the entire frets of the young man she had just met, and Edmund showed her just how much he valued Leola with that simple reply. No arguments, no why's or why not's, it just was.

Betty seemed just as intrigued by Edmund and his new history as he was about her. Edmund watched her interaction with Leola as they walked back to her home from dinner. She was simple, mild mannered, and had just a little more southern than she did city. He could tell she was well educated and intelligent given how well she documented their conversations. He also noticed how Leola kept saying, "see I told you" as they walked in front of him, just out of earshot.

As they began to walk up the steps of Leola's covered porch, Leola quickly turned around and faced them both. She told them both goodnight and scurried to her room with nothing more than a hum and a giggle under her breath.

"She told you I was coming didn't she?" Edmund asked.

"Yep, three weeks ago she called and said I needed to be here to meet somebody who would need some historical guidance, and she made me an offer I couldn't refuse," Betty said.

"Really," Edmund said with gusto.

"Free room and board for the week in exchange for my guidance and a history lesson. Now don't argue with her; you know she's right and she isn't able to tour you around. I'll help you get where you need to go, and I'm not going to press you on anything so please don't get that idea. I'm not that kind of lady," Betty said with a smirk.

Edmund opened his mouth to speak, but no words could come to mind. He was speechless. The only mother he'd known for years had set him up, and Betty was brilliant and beautiful on top of all that.

"Well, with that, I'll see you at breakfast. I'm thinking parts of this story sound familiar, and I know where to look tomorrow to help you find the documents. So, goodnight Edmund," Betty said.

"Goodnight, Betty," Edmund said as she dashed through the front door and gracefully made her way up the stairs.

Edmund stood in shock on the porch. He wasn't ready to sleep, so he took an about face and headed back down the stairs. He went into Leola's garden where he could see the mountains, and could think.

"Well Dad, this isn't how I expected this to go," Edmund began to speak into the crisp night sky. "So, just not too many more surprises; okay old man? And Dad, I'm sorry I gave up on you. I had no idea, but you knew that already."

It took him a few minutes to regain his composure. He walked around the dimly lit gardens lost in all he had learned over the past few days.
He had always led a quiet life so all of this attention was more than he thought he could handle. His emotions began to get the best of him as he pondered all that his father had left for him. His tears watered the ground that had began to crunch from the winter's thick evening frost. He needed time to process on his own with no one but the crickets and the bullfrogs listening. It wasn't long before the back porch light came on, and he heard the familiar sound of the creek of the screen door on the back porch.

"Edmund?" Leola called out to him as if calling a child home for dinner.

"I'm fine," he said, as he wiped the tears from his cheeks.

"Oh, I'm sorry Sweetie, I just wanted to say thank you for the best night of my life; well, in a long time," Leola said.

Edmund turned toward her, and she could see his dimly lit face from the porch lights glow as he approached the back porch. She could see the red puffy eyes and knew he had been crying.

"Oh honey, come here," she said.

Edmund picked up his pace and ran to her as she met him in the yard. Her hug was what he needed; he cried without reserve. His raw emotion ran down the house coat Leola adorned. She hugged him in a tight embrace until his sobs lessened and his tears were almost gone.

"Now, dry your eyes. You've got a lot to learn about this town tomorrow. Now, I'm sorry I didn't tell you about her, but you wouldn't have come. She's a good girl. I wouldn't put you in any danger. I trust her just as much as I trust you. She knows more about this town than I could tell you, and she's not biased. She sees it from all sides. I can't tell you the history I've learned from her, things I never knew. I wouldn't lead you wrong, but I had no idea about the property or the money. I just knew your family was strategic with everything that happened around the general store," Leola reassured him.

"I know; it's just been a lot all at one time. And being set up, well, that I wasn't expecting," Edmund replied.

"Ah, so I did see what I thought I saw." Leola said with a smile.

"Maybe," Edmund began. "And, I'll ask you not to spur it on any further, okay? She is beautiful, but I'm emotionally and mentally exhausted."

"Oh, alright. I'll take a maybe, and I'll leave it alone. I promise," Leola said like a proud mother would. "Now, go to bed. It's been a long day."

The screen door creaked as they went inside. One by one, the lights went off in the B&B as Edmund climbed the stairs to his room.

Betty lay in tears in her guest bedroom: Butterflies, excitement and happy tears.

Leola may have promised to no further meddle in the spark she saw, but she did place their backyard conversation conveniently underneath Betty's single pane picture window, knowing she would hear every word.

Especially that "Maybe."

Chapter Twelve

The Red Barn

The eggs and sizzle of bacon woke Edmund up. He wished that more mornings started out this way- homemade breakfast instead of a granola bar. He knew it was early, but that really didn't matter today. He reveled in all that happened at dinner last night, and the overpowering emotions he felt in the gardens. He didn't realize that having someone on his side was really what he needed until then. Everyone else was on his dad's side. He was excited to begin to form the missing pieces of confirmed history to the rest of the story today. Betty's help would be great he thought if she does know as much as Leola says she does. He took his time getting ready. He knew the town hall places wouldn't open until eight thirty, and it was shortly after seven he thought. He was combing his hair in the bathroom when he began to hear conversations downstairs about the mine, and where they would go today. He was self-assured that Leola had made a good choice. And then she said Anna. He had only mentioned her name once or twice, but that's when he decided he had better get to breakfast.

"I hope my eggs aren't cold," Edmund said.

"Child, I know you better than I know myself. I don't start cooking your eggs until I hear the toothbrush clank on the sink," Leola said, as she slid two perfectly cooked sunny side up cooked eggs onto his plate.

"Why thank you," Edmund said as he sat down across from Betty.

"Good mornin," he said to Betty as he put his napkin in his lap.

"Good Mornin," Betty said as she lifted her eyes from her notes from dinner last night.

"So, there are a few documents and news articles. I mean dozens, but they are there surrounding the days and months before they released the flood waters. The town historian has tried to catalog every detail with timelines and maps. I think I can show you where your grandfather's store was on the maps! I know I can! We should be able to get a handle on that fairly quickly."

"And what about Anna? Why were you talking about her?" Edmund asked.

"Well isn't she the big unknown? There's got to be more to her than just running off and eloping with her war time hero and falling off the face of the planet," Betty replied.

"I just hope to learn who she was, and where she is If she is even still alive," Edmund said.

"Well, good. We've got a goal. It will take some time to find out about her though; all of the documents aren't online yet, It's old time research, papers taped in books or on microfiche. That isn't the top priority today though. I'd like to know where you would like to start. This is your history lesson, not mine," Betty stated inquisitively.

"Well, I'd like to know where the property is in the county so can we go there first," Edmund began.

"Sure, it's the farthest from town so that will be easy. It should take less time here than it does in Raleigh," Betty said.

As soon as breakfast was done they packed their notes, the will instructions, probate papers, and his father's box, and headed over to the new government building just outside of downtown. The Register of Deeds office was there.

The awkward silence of butterflies filled the ten-minute car ride until Edmund asked where she was from. "Banner Elk," she told him. "They're a drinking town with a skiing problem."

Her reply gave Edmund enough confidence that this day wouldn't be boring. She was sharp.

The new building was efficient with solid technology Edmund wasn't expecting. They were greeted by a very friendly staff who began to explain the process of updating the deeds, and what paperwork needed to be completed. Edmund handed over the paperwork from the closed meeting with the judge; all of the paperwork was already completed in the packet. Edmund hadn't even looked through the packet. He had been so overwhelmed with the history of his father that he failed to realize that he already had the address of his father's house.

He turned around in disbelief to show Betty who he figured was standing behind him. She wasn't. She was chatting with the Town Historian in the hallway. About that time she pointed towards him, to identify him to her, and he acknowledged with a smile and a wave. He asked for a moment, but the associate told him he was done for the day. He would have to come back and pick up the official papers in a few days, but here was a copy of the work report so he could have the information that was transferred over to him.

He had in hand his name on a property. A property he never knew existed:
1457 Elf School Hollow Road
Elf, North Carolina.

He thanked the attendant; placed his paperwork back in his file and was relieved that this part was over. He gently closed the door as he left, and walked in on Betty getting a play by play on what books she would need from the Historical Society.

Betty introduced the two, "Edmund, this is Diane Sweeney, the Town Historian we spoke of."

"Edmund, I've heard the stories of your grandfather's store for years. It's nice to meet someone in the next generation! And might I add, you do have his eyes." Diane began.

Edmund blushed and was taken back to that black and white photo his dad had when he was a child. She was right; he did have his grandfather's eyes. Diane began to lie out where things would be in the historical society, and said she would be along shortly to let them in. Diane was making sure the Judge knew his private chamber at the old courthouse would be closed for a while for the renovations; then she would be right over.

Edmund and Betty walked back to the car where he could only think of one thing to say, "Well, I have a house. I just hope it's better than that other property."

Betty laughed as she could only imagine what the other property was really like, the brief description he gave at dinner left little to the imagination when "dump" and 'torn down" were the main part of its description.

"Well, would you like to find out?" Betty asked. "It's going to be a few minutes before Diane can get there; I'm sure it isn't far. What's the address?"

"It's on Elm School Hollow Road, so I'd assume by the Old Elf School," Edmund replied.

"So you do know at least some landmarks," Betty smirked as she waited for his reply.

Edmund said, "Yes, it's the running joke at the office that I came from the land of elves, and that's why I'm so weird."

"You are not weird," Betty replied. "So, let's go. Let's see what your house is like."

The drive wasn't far from where they were. Just off of US 64 just outside of town a small brick schoolhouse stood where many a child got an education. It had been sold many times over, and was now someone's home, however; people would come for miles to say they sat with the elves that guard the flagpole.

The road bore to the right as the trees began to line the drive. The mailbox was broken and the numbers were barely visible, but this was his new 'home'. As they rounded the corner the edge of a red barn with a dark roof came into view. Nice, he thought, he could have a barn along with his house. Much to his surprise at the end of the long drive there only sat a large red barn with doors that had been shut for years. It appeared to be a converted dairy barn with windows on one side that faced out to the lake. Edmund put the car in park and just shook his head in disgust with the outward appearance. The grass hadn't been cut in years, and the weeds were taller than the car.

"Look, you don't have to go in there. There's no telling what will be in there," Edmund said in fear of the insanity he knew demented his father.

Please Betty replied, "Are you scared because your history is in there? Or are you scared that I'll have to wrangle a bear?"

She had put him in his place, She already knew the answer, but wanted to see just how Edmund would answer.

"Alright then, we can go together, okay?" Edmund replied.

"That's more like it! I'm here for a mystery, not to sit in a car and wonder what's in there. Besides, if the bear gets you first, I can go get you help, or a hearse. You know, just in case," Betty replied with a grin.

"At least let me go first." Edmund said trying to regain a small bit of his ego.

"So now you are trying to be all Knight in shining armor; I see," Betty replied.

"Maybe," he said. "I've got some boots in the trunk; I can't mess up my loafers." He popped the trunk to see his boots and his grandfather's box. He changed his shoes, picked up the box and began heading towards the barn. Betty was waiting for him. She would let him go first so as not to bruise his ego any further.

As Edmund and Betty slowly made their way closer to the structure, a paved sidewalk could be seen around the edge of the barn. Edmund tried to take bigger steps to get out of the grass quicker, but remembered Betty was behind him about the time he reached the sidewalk. He turned around to extend his hand to help her. It was the first time he had intentionally reached for her. With a blushing smile, she placed her hand in his for the last few steps.

Edmund was surprised. The back side of the barn appeared to resemble a house more than a barn, The windows filled the southern side of the house, but the dust didn't allow for much of a view to what was inside. A small stoop showed wear and tear from years of the lakes storms, but the door appeared to be solid considering it hadn't been used in quite some time. He began to look through the box for the keys hoping one would fit the door.

The keys jingled in his hand as he pulled them out of the box. He wasn't sure he was prepared for all of the mental chaos he knew he would find. He hesitated as he swirled the keys around his index finger. He took a deep breath, looking at the keys he saw a red square taped to one of the keys with a faint 'B' in his father's handwriting.

Barn.

Red Barn.

He picked that key and said, "Well, here goes nothing," as he stuck the key in the lock.

It fit.

Chapter Thirteen

July 1st, 1942

James Ellington was barely sixteen. He had made it his mission to fill the new lake with fish. Some were brought in with the release of the initial waters, but he wanted to make sure his favorite fish, the catfish, would be in the new waters that covered his old homestead. He had been fishing and catching catfish for a few weeks and releasing them in the early morning hours the following day. Today was no different. He was walking to his favorite cove to release his catch from the night before. He cleared the last knoll to see a woman walking into the lake. He started screaming at her, "Hey! Hey! What are you doing? Stop!" He dropped the bucket of catfish and ran as fast as he could. He was splashing in the waters edge as her head sank beneath the weight of the waters.

She never turned around. She never heard a word he said. She could only hear the waters calling to her, begging her to join the ghosts that they surrounded.

He reached her limp body and began to scream for help. In shock of what he had seen, and not knowing what to do, he carried her to the nearest house begging for help. The blue lips of her body stuck in his mind. He just hoped he got her to someone who would help her in time.

****

Once Betty and Edmund made their way inside, they were both surprised over what they saw. The barn had been converted into a one large great room with a bedroom off to one side. It was a simple view he wasn't expecting. The furniture was from the seventies, and appeared to be the furniture from his old home, from what he could remember. He meandered through a relatively neat kitchen and onto a large dining room table where mail had been sorted for years. He froze in fear of what was on the table, and the fear of what he would find in the bedroom. Betty saw his reaction and tried her best to redirect his attention to the second floor.

"Edmund, check out the loft! What a window!" Betty exclaimed.

Edmund nodded, acknowledging the view and the sun light that was bellowing through the dust covered window.

"Can we go to town now? I just need to look through something that's organized before I tackle this." Edmund said.

"Sure. How about I walk into the bedroom just to see what's in there. You don't have to look. Would that be okay?" Betty asked.

"Fine." Edmund said with a heavy sigh.

Betty walked over the creaking floors to the half opened door of the bedroom. Edmund was looking casually through the cabinets knowing all of the food would have to be thrown out. The dates on the cans ranged from 1995 to 2007. He began to feel overwhelmed when he heard Betty calling him.

"Edmund, Do you remember anything about your bedroom when you were a kid?" Betty asked with an inquisitive tone.

"Four post full size bed, topped with a handmade..." Edmund began.

"Quilt?" Betty finished his sentence.

"Yes, we lived by the mill, and my mom would always go buy scraps of fabric. She made quilts until she died. I kept the last one. I hated washing it; it was the only thing that smelled of her for a very long time. I kept it on my bed when I left for the military," Edmund said reminiscing.

"Did you have any posters on the wall?" Betty questioned. Edmund stopped his cabinet searching and turned towards the bedroom.

"Uncle Sam" Edmund said, as he walked in to see that his father had recreated his bedroom in his barn just as he had left it when he left for the Army.

"Can we leave now? Please," Edmund asked.

"You are driving, of course we can. Let's go," Betty said reassuringly.

Edmund quickly turned and headed for the door. Betty took a moment to take in everything that was around her. The design of a man who did everything he could to preserve the moment in life before his mental illness completely took over and his 'family' life ended.

"Are you coming?" Edmund called from the door.

"Yep, just taking it all in. It really gives me perspective on who your father was, you know?" Betty asked.

"Sort of, I really lost him when I left for the Army. He was never the same after my mom died. I wish I would have known all of this," Edmund replied.

"It wouldn't mean as much today if you knew. Now, let's go," Betty said as she headed for the car.

They drove with small chatter surrounding the Red Barn, and how impressed they were with how Porter had recreated to the last detail his bedroom. How organized things were to be as far along as his dementia was. The cans were in lines in the cabinet, the towels were neatly stacked, the living room was almost not used. That's when

Edmund realized his father recreated their old house, and had lived in the small apartment where it was nothing but a continuous disaster. He wanted this part to be perfect. That's why the barn was there.

Edmund and Betty arrived at the Hayesville Historical Society around nine, and Diane could be heard in the back moving boxes and pulling books from the shelves. She honestly was just as excited about this piece of history, as they were to fill in the gaps.

"Betty, can you and Mr. Wise come back here and help me?" Diane called from the back of the pale yellow building.

"Of course! We are on the way," Betty said.

Edmund was in awe of all of the historical documents, photos, quilts, and artifacts that had been acquired over many, many years inside the Society's building. Each room was ornately detailed with information concerning valuable parts of Hayesville's history. He slowly walked through the quilt displays and into the room that held all of the news articles concerning the TVA, the Tusquittee boys, and pictures of the downtown and parts of Hayesville from as far back as there was a camera to take photos. Maps covered large wall spaces showing the original maps of the fertile land now covered by Lake Chatuge. He stood there in shock at how much land really was under the lake.

"I told you I would show you that, but right now, I need your help back here, okay?" Betty reminded him as she popped her head back into the room he was waylaid in.

"Sorry. There's just so much here. I never knew," Edmund replied as he followed Betty down a hallway and into a room filled with military memorabilia.

"This just scratches the surface. There is so much more, there just isn't enough space," Diane informed him.

"We've tried to display the most important pieces, but there is so much more we just don't have enough room to display it all. Now, this book has the newspaper clippings of your grandfather's obituary. And this is the story of the man who tried to save him," Diane said.

Edmund coughed; it was fake and Diane knew it. She could read people like you can read a book. She knew something wasn't right.

"How many months are in this book? And would it have information on weddings as well? No one really questioned my grandfather's death and this hero? He wasn't a hero." Edmund's raw emotions began to show themselves.

"Everything is chronologically placed in these books. I've been doing this since I was a little girl. This book holds January 1942- May 1943. We don't have every article, but there are some wedding notifications and obituaries that were saved. We can look through them, but I want to know about this 'not a hero' business. What's the *real* story?

For the next hour Edmund, Betty and Diane rehashed everything Edmund had learned in the last few days: the mine, the fire, the shots, the cover up. Diane was amazed that it was so well planned and thought through by all three families so quickly, and that the cover up lasted so long without anyone saying anything different.

They were looking through the book of newspaper articles and at Layton Wise's obituary. Edmund read over and over the few lines that were written when he finally could stand it no longer and pointed at Anna's name.

"Who was she?" Edmund asked with a heavy heart.

"I think you mean who *is* she?" Diane said.

Edmund and Betty's eyes lit up. He wasn't the only living Wise! There was someone else.

Anna.

Chapter Fourteen

July 1st, 1942

Dr. Calvin came out of the bedroom with a stern but sad look to a scared sixteen year old and the Jackson family hovering around the kitchen table. In a strange twist of fate, the Ellington boy brought her right to the house where her brother now lived. She was unrecognizable to him as her lifeless body was carried in the back bedroom, and at such a young age, he was shielded from most of it. Mrs. Jackson knew Porter couldn't handle the thought of his sister being dead; he had just started to get back to a normal sense of himself.

"Is she alive? Is she?" The Ellington boy began to scream at the doctor.

"Yes, but just barely. I don't know if the baby will survive, though," Dr. Calvin replied.

"Baby? What Baby!" Mrs. Jackson said. She sat down as not to pass out from sheer shock and the overwhelming emotions she was having.

"It appears that she is about six to seven months along. It is possible. She got married in January, right?" The doctor asked.

"Yes, but her husband died. Lord, she thought she couldn't do it on her own. Blessed be! Anna!" Mrs. Jackson moaned through tears of grief.

"You've got to save her; she is all that boy's got left, Doc. You've got to save her!" Mr. Jackson said as he was consoling his wife.

"I'll try my best, but I'm really not sure that either of them will make it. She's got to want to make it. You did good, Son. You did more than any of us could ask. Don't you ever doubt that, you hear?" The doctor said.

"Yes, sir," Ellington said.

"Now, help me get her in my car. I'm going to have to take her to the hospital if she is ever going to make it."

For weeks Anna lay in a hospital bed in a coma. Her belly grew, but the doctors could not hear or feel movement from the baby. Soon, her water broke, and a stillborn infant boy was delivered. They named him Jeffrey Layton Faulk. He was buried on the island in a small grave where the original Wise plot was. Mrs. Jackson didn't know that the bodies of her friend, husband and their children were in a corundum mine, so taking him there would have given away part of the secluded secrets Mr. Jackson fought so hard to keep.

Months went by. Years came and went, with little to no improvement with Anna. She was alert enough to eat, but had no clue who she was, or what life she had, or that she was a mother to a baby boy she would never hear cry.

****

November 7, 1987

"Hello?" Porter answered the phone.

"I see. I'll be there shortly. Thank you, goodbye," Porter replied as he hung up the phone.

He began to beat his hands on his head almost in a psychotic episode. Edmund remembered hearing tires squealing down the road, but not much else.

It was the time his father's dementia "started".
It was the day Anna woke up.

The nurses and doctors at the rest home had told him a few weeks ago that they believed some of the connections in Anna's brain were starting to reconnect. It wasn't unheard of, but it wasn't common. The nurse on the other end of the phone line told Porter that Anna had been having a nightmare and fell out of bed. When she did, she hit her head on the night stand at her bedside table. After hearing her initial screams, she only asked for one thing:

Jeffery.

She remembered the love of her life.

"Isn't he home from the war?"
"He said he was coming for me."
"Has Jeffrey written you to say when he can make it from Asheville?"

She never questioned why she was in a hospital bed, or where the baby was. She just wanted Jeffery.

Until the day Porter died he saw Anna.

Anna never knew who he was, but she knew he wasn't Jeffery. The only Porter she knew was a small boy in overalls. No matter how many times he tried to tell her who he was she never made the connection.

Every November Porter would sneak into the old mine and lay a single rose on her grave. He'd put the key back under the pillow in a new bottle. It's when Anna died to him. He did that for ten years, until he couldn't remember where his "other" property was.

~~~~~~~~~

December 23, 2015

Edmund sat in shock; he wasn't alone. In an instant, he stood up and without saying a word he walked out of the building. Betty and Diane sat shocked, but continued to look for more information and talk about the barn, the box, and the locket.

Edmund ran through the brisk air to the bank.

"I need to speak with the manager. Now," Edmund demanded.

The teller picked up the phone and pointed towards the office where Mr. Gibbs was seated. Edmund walked in the door of his office and slammed it shut.

"You knew. You knew didn't you," he barked at Gibbs.

"Knew what?" Gibbs asked.

"About Anna. You knew about Anna, that's why you said you were taking care of my *family*. Right? Please tell me I am right," Edmund said.

"Yes, I knew about Anna. Your father would make deposits every January or February and would split them evenly. Anna also has a large sum of money in her account, and it pays for her care. Every month, the same amount is withdrawn," Gibbs replied.

"Where is she? Who gets the money? Where can I find her?" Edmund asked in a panic.

"Son, she's got to be well into her nineties now. She's taken care of. Don't you have the statements? Your dad always kept the statements. It should be on there," Gibbs replied.

"The papers! He did keep them! Thank you, Mr. Gibbs, Thank you," Edmund said, as he reached across the table to shake his hand.

After shaking hands, Edmund opened the door and headed for the front of the bank.

"Son have you..." He could hear Gibbs asking him before he made it to the door.

"Not yet." Edmund replied. He knew what he was asking about; if he had found the source of the money.

With renewed hope he dashed back to the historical society. Diane had pulled the news clippings about Anna's drowning just so Edmund could lay his eyes on it.

"Well, I guess I'm going to have to write up something on this for the historical facts," Diane said.

" I've already had that done for you. You can have a copy of her notes, when we are done with them," Edmund replied.

Betty began to blush; he really trusted her and now she knew it. "Where to from here, Sherlock?" Betty asked.

"The dining room table," Edmund replied.

Edmund was so excited he barely said two words on the drive back to the barn. He was out of the car almost before the car was fully in park. Betty was shocked to see this much gusto, and she clapped to herself out of sheer joy knowing part of this mystery was minutes from being solved.

Edmund was in the house and at the dining room table before Betty could even get to the door. She entered to see him looking through the papers, stack by stack until he found her stack. Anna's papers had been neatly placed in stacks on one side of the table, while Porter's were on the other. Several years worth of statements from a nursing home in Macon County confirmed where she was. She wasn't far from the old Jackson homestead.

"I know where she is! I know!" Edmund shouted with exhilaration.

"Okay! Let's go," Betty said, almost automatically knowing that would be what was next.

"Right. Okay, Let's go see Anna!" Edmund exclaimed happily.

Edmund and Betty used the next hour to talk about each other, and not the last week of excitement in Edmund's life. They talked about Edmund's military career, his job at the law firm, his life in Raleigh. All normal things that two people who were just getting to know each other would.

Anna told him of her childhood, happy and sweet. She was an only child with two great parents who allowed her to see parts of the U.S. during the summer while she was out of school. She was born and raised in a small town of Crossnore, North Carolina. After graduation from Appalachian State University, she settled into Banner Elk, a little farther north and west from hometown. She worked at a small country store to keep the bills paid, and also worked a in freelance atmosphere helping people with family history searches, land deed confirmations, and was regularly commissioned to draw or paint artwork varying from old cars to landscapes. It was enough for her; it was what she enjoyed.

"I was almost married once," Betty said out of the blue.

"Really. Did he leave you at the altar?" Edmund asked.

"Quite literally," Betty began, "He ran off with my best friend. They've got four kids now. Man you should have seen the look on his mother's face when he walked her back down the aisle and not me. I had made it to the altar after she and two of my bride's maids, and the pastor said 'dearly beloved'. He was crying, she was crying, I just thought they were happy. Turns out, they had been in love for years and had started dating just weeks before. They thought it would be a fling, I guess, but when love brings two people together, you just can't stop fate."

"Wow. I can't believe he actually walked her back down the aisle! Ha!" Edmund replied.

"Yep. Hand in hand. And she handed me her bouquet. Like I knew what to do with it!" Betty said with a laugh, "So, I turned around looked at a church full of people and said, "I guess that thats over." They were already gasping, and in shock. I was just glad we didn't say 'I do'. They are so happy now. I've even had dinner with them. We've made up. It took years, but I couldn't let the only friend I ever really had walk out of my life over a man. We don't talk much, but it is civil. We really are just on two opposite ends of the spectrum. All her conversations are about her kids, and all of mine are about history, and finding lost loved ones." Betty sighed.

"So is that why you spend so much time researching history? Are you afraid of your future?" Edmund asked.

"Well I do believe that is the most physiological question I've heard you ask since we met. No, I'm not afraid of my future. I just haven't found anyone who enjoys it as much as I do. And until then, it's me and the books,." Betty said.

Edmund smirked and laughed under his breath. Her desire to just be with the books is how he felt about his cases at the law firm. It just kept him busy. Not that it was what he wanted to do with his life, but it is what he had settled into. She apparently had done the same.

It wasn't long before they arrived at the rest home. Edmund and Betty walked in to be greeted by an orderly. She directed the pair to a room down the east wing where they would find Anna.

When he entered the room he saw a beautiful ninety-five year old Anna sleeping. Her hair was white and long, her skin seemed frail, and her breath seemed labored. Betty stayed close to the door hoping that Anna would wake up even if for only a few minutes. Edmund stood there watching her sleep. He saw a resemblance of his father in her face, yet her beauty was still visible. Even with all she had been through she was never tarnished.

Edmund sat at the foot of her bed to see if she would gently arise from her slumber. He placed his hand on her knee as she began to awake. The nurse had told him at the nurses station that she has always asked for Jeffrey, and she still thought it was 1942. He had resolved within himself that whatever she called him, he would be.

"Anna" Edmund said quietly as she began to stir.

"Jeffery, Jeffery! Is that you? You found me! Can we go home? I'm ready to go home," Anna said. Her frail body sat up in the bed and he reached in for an embrace. Edmund held her as she told him how much she loved him, and missed him, and she was glad his tour was so short. She actually thought it was still 1942.

He assured her that it was for the best that she stay here a while longer, that he had things he had to get ready before she could come home. She seemed to understand, but she was so glad that her 'Jeffrey' was home. It wasn't long before Anna saw Betty standing at the edge of the door. A single tear had rolled down her cheek, as Anna asked the 'nurse' to come in. Betty sat on the other side of the foot of the bed and listened to Anna tell her story of how she and Jeffrey met.

"I was at my daddy's store one day, and this handsome boy came bouncing in the door looking for a pack of smokes with some of his pals. I told him if smokes is what he wants smokes is what he'll get, but it would ruin his beautiful smile. His pals snickered at the door that I would say such a thing, but I guess they didn't know who they were dealing with. I've always been a pistol. Well, wouldn't you know it, he told me if I'd go out with him

143

he'd never buy smokes again. That was just a couple of weeks before we got married. I swooned over him, and he treated me like a queen. I told him all I wanted was to be his wife, before he went off to war. He told me, 'I was his won one', and that I was the catch, not him. That's when we planned our getaway and that we would run off and tells no one. It was heaven," Anna said.

By this time, the *real* nurse was standing at the door crying like a baby. It was the most cognitive sense Anna had ever made. Anna stroked Edmunds cheeks, ran her fingers through his hair, and told him it was time for a haircut.

He assured her it would be okay, and he would get one but that it would be a bit before she could go home with him.

"Jeffrey, do you know where my locket is? I can't seem to find it," Anna asked.

"I do, I know right where it is, give me just a minute," Edmund replied.

"Of course, my love." Anna said.

Edmund leaned in and gave Anna a gentle kiss on the forehead, and he could see the blush rising in her cheeks.

"I love you, Anna" Edmund softly said.

"I love you, too." Anna replied

He calmly walked out of the room, but then ran down the corridor out of the east wing. The locket was still in his Grandfather's box in his car. He fumbled with the keys to open the trunk, frantically searching through the box for the locket. He saw the heart just as he heard Betty calling for him.

"Edmund! Edmund! Hurry! They think she is dying! Hurry Edmund", Betty frantically screamed from the door.

He snatched the locket and ran as fast as he could, nurses and aides parting to the side of the hall as he ran by them. He entered Anna's room to see that they had placed an oxygen mask on her. Anna's breathing was suddenly more labored and her color wasn't as good as it was just moments before.

"I told you I knew where it was. Here my dear." Edmund said to Anna as he placed the locket in her hand. She began to cry tears of joy. Edmund began to console her, and crawled into the bed to lie beside her. He told her over and over that she was loved, and that it was okay to go "'Home'".

With her locket clinched tightly in one hand, Edmund curled beside her holding the other, and Betty sitting by her feet, just hours after her 'Jeffrey' returned, Anna peacefully passed away in Edmund's arms.

The nurse came in to ask if he knew which funeral home would be handling the arrangements so they could arrange for transportation for her body. Edmund thought and began to shake his head, "Is there one close to Lake Nantahala?" he asked.

The nurse nodded and gave him the business card for the funeral director.

He made the call to them, explained his plan, which they agreed to. A family plot was acceptable for burial even if it was in a corundum mine. The director asked about flowers for the spread, and what casket he would be interested in.

Edmund's reply was simple, "She deserves the finest wooden casket you have with the most beautiful spread of red roses a florist can make." It truly is what she deserved.

December 27th, 2015

Anna Wise Faulk was laid to rest with most of her family in the mine. The Tomlin and Jackson families were there as well as Leola and Betty. The sweet service was short with memories and tales of moonshining, the store, and finally telling both families what really happened that cold January morning in 1942.

Before Edmund locked the mine, he took the rose from his lapel, and laid it on top of the casket. With a gentle touch he said goodbye. He walked out into the small corridor, pushed the door shut and locked the mine for the final time.

Betty & Edmund returned to the Red Barn. Edmund had gotten the power turned on and the grass cut by a neighbor so it was warm and more functional when they arrived. He and Betty began sorting through the papers, tossing what was too old, and filing what was Anna's for her probate for her estate. They were working on the last stack when Betty heard something she wasn't expecting.

"Thank you," Edmund said.

"You are welcome. This has honestly been amazing for me. I've been so emotionally charged with everything. It's helped me get through some of my grief that I had built up over so many years of just burying it," Betty replied.

"I feel the same way. So much pain and anger that had been nagging me for so long; it seems like nothing now. So, what's next?" Edmund asked.

"You mean the kitchen or the loft?" Betty replied. "Yes, um, yes I guess, which room?

"No Betty, what's next with us? My mystery is all but solved, and well, I'd really like to see you again outside of this perfect storm." Edmund said.

"I'd like to see you too. But let's tackle the loft first, okay?"

Edmund's butterflies turned to a sense of peace. He had said what he wanted to say days ago, and he was glad to see that she felt the same way.

The loft was filled with boxes of random items: canning jars, scales, an antique four post bed, a stack of quilts, and shelves that lined either side of the large picture window. Betty began to clean the window from the layers of dust as Edmund sorted through the boxes.

"Why would he have all this random crap? I mean look at this! Stacks and stacks of glass bottles, parts and pieces of antique weights. I just don't get it!" Edmund said with a laugh.

"Maybe it would have something to do with this," Betty said.

Edmund saw her standing by the window looking at one of the several jars that were on the shelves beside the picture window.

"What is it?" Edmund asked as he tried to get up from the floor surrounded by boxes of small glass bottles.

"I think it's gold," Betty said.

"What? Gold? No way!" Edmund replied.

"Look, there are more of them. They each have a year on them! I swear it's gold!" Betty began to shriek.

"Here! Open one. See if I'm right!" she said.

Edmund took the perfume size bottle in his hands. It was dated February 1988. He popped the small cork, and saw thousands of tiny flakes of gold filling two thirds of the bottle.

"How many more jars are there?" Edmund asked.

"I don't know, but I think I know where they came from," Betty said.

Without thinking she quickly swirled the room, saw a panning bowl, grabbed it and flew down the stairs.

"Wait! What is it? Where are you going?" Edmund yelled.

"Hurry! You'll see!" she cried.

Edmund made it out the door to see her running to the lake shore. He picked up his pace, and was able to see her swirling the bright orange dirt that was more visible in the winter time with the frigid waters.

In the winter, the lake levels have always been reduced to create energy, and it was the only time you were able to walk out so far on the shore and look for things from the valley. He had known that for years, but just had not put two and two together that this is what his father had been doing.

The dirt swirled in the pan and Betty intently told him, "There was always a rumor that there was a gold mine in the valley. For years small flecks were found in random places, but they weren't enough for anyone to really think anything of it. The mine was small, but there would be small pockets of gold that were found back in the 20's. They finally stopped in the 30's because it had been so long since anyone had found anything. I bet when they blew up the mine they actually released a larger pocket." she said.

"Oh my Gosh. And the only time you could find anything was in the winter. That's why he was always sick; he was out here looking for gold!" Edmund exclaimed.

"And he found it! Look Edmund!" Betty held the pan up for him to see hundreds of specks of gold. Gold that could only be seen in the winter when the lake receded.

Chapter Fifteen

June 30th, 2017

Betty and Edmund had casually been dating for little over a year before they really started talking about the future, and what it would look like. They had both made a clear distinction that they had no desire to be with anyone else. Edmund still worked for Lisa at the law firm in Raleigh at least part time every month. He spent half of his time there, and half of his time in Hayesville working on repairing and restoring the old barn. Betty would come and help on the weekends, but she spent most of her time with Leola learning how to cook. She was getting there!

He was a few days from heading back to Hayesville when he went to Cameron Village in Raleigh one day for lunch. He was meandering through the antique stores looking for something for Betty. He came across an antique jewelry counter and stood there looking at all of the beautiful pieces. The antique broaches were magnificent; He wanted to get Betty something unique, but he wasn't quite sure what he wanted. He had been standing at the counter long enough for the owner of the store to walk back to him.

"Sir, can I help you?" the lady asked.

"I want to say I love you, but I don't want to say I love you with a diamond. She doesn't like diamonds." Edmund replied.

"Come with me," she said.

She led Edmund to a back room where she had trays and trays of jewelry of all different kinds.

"Now, this I love you, is this *the* I love you?" she asked.

"Yes, I think it is," Edmund replied.

"But she doesn't like diamonds?"

"She doesn't like diamonds. The last one she had left her at the altar," Edmund replied.

"Ah. so is she bold? Is she quiet? Is she enchanting?" the storeowner asked.

"She's all of those. How do you put that in a ring?" Edmund questioned.

"It's easy. When you see it, you'll know," she began, "Now, have a seat, I'll be right back.".

"She's an original. It can't be a reproduction," Edmund shouted to her.

"I figured that. Hang on, I've got just the tray. I just have to find it."

She was walking back and forth amongst the shelves when Edmund heard a giggle from the back. She approached with three trays and a great big smile.

"Now, there's lots of options in lots of a price ranges. What's your budget?" She asked.

"It's not about the budget; it's about the right one," he said.

For an hour Edmund peered over the three trays. He had learned some about gold and gems since finding the bottles of gold in the loft. He looked for flaws, the cut, the clarity. For a while the storeowner stood with him until she had other customers come in.

"I need to go help them, are you okay here?" she asked.

Edmund had finished two of the trays, and was beginning to look through the third one, "yep" he said as he picked up the next ring.

She returned thirty minutes later apologizing for taking so long, when she realized he had found the one. The look on his face was different. He was inspecting every detail over and over when he turned to her and said, "Tell me about this one."

"This piece came from an estate of a local debutante. Her husband told her she was always the gem that no one saw. When he found this emerald it was in a flawed class because of the embedded ruby. But that is what makes it so special; it's small but noticeable. Under light the red shines in the shape of a heart that can faintly be seen on the facets of the ring. Other than the flawed ruby the stone is a brilliant color green set in 14k gold. The gold is strong but soft. What else can I tell you about it?" she asked.

"How quickly can you get it sized to 6 & 1/4?" he replied.

August 21st, 2017

Edmund could hardly contain himself. He knew just how special this was going to be. The weather had panned out to be a small fog of a morning, which began to clear by noon. He had helped Betty setup a telescope, a camera, and a video camera so that she could go through every moment of the day.

He had also invited the Tomlins, the Jacksons and the Gibbs families as well as his beloved Leola. None of them knew what was really happening. They all thought they were there to see a clear view of the solar eclipse from the shore of the lake.

As the eclipse began around 1:30 the edges of the moon began to overtake the brightness of the sun.

Edmund told Betty, "You and I, we are like the moon and the sun today. We just kind of fit together."

Betty told him, "You are right, sometimes we are complete opposites, but when we are together I swear it's magical."

Edmund just smiled and walked over to talk with some of his guests. It was the first time any of them had been to the barn, and he had restored it to the best of his ability to meet his needs.

He quietly moved Leola's chair close to Betty, and told her this would be the best seat in the house, and she didn't need to miss it. Leola's face lit up; she knew.

"Are you?" she asked quietly.

"Maybe." he replied with a smirk.

By 2:15 the birds and insects had begun to sing as if it were nearing dusk. Betty was constantly taking photos and recording and hopping from the telescope to the camera. Edmund was pleased to see her so happy, but the butterflies were beginning to overwhelm him. Leola took his hand to calm him.

At 2:36, the rays from the sun began to glimmer in a circular motion on the mountains, the lake and the ground.

At 2:38 the totality phase of the eclipse began. It was as if dusk had set in in a moments notice. Edmund announced everyone could remove their glasses so they could see the sun. It was too dark with the glasses on to see anything during the totality phase.

Edmund had timed it. He knew how long before the diamond ring phase would occur: when the moon had just moved from totality and the shape of a ring appeared.

Betty was steadily looking at the telescope when she said, "I see it! I see the diamond ring!"

She moved over to the video camera to make sure it was in view. When Edmund saw that she was completely focused he knelt on one knee in front of the camera and held the ring up in front of the lens.

"Wait, I can't see the ring, It's out of focus," Betty said.

It was loud enough and odd enough that it caught the attention of everyone, and they all turned to see what it was she was having an issue with.

She zoomed the camera out to see the emerald ring come into focus. She immediately stood up, put her hands on her cheeks, and began to squeal.

"Will you marry me?" Edmund asked.

Betty took just a second and replied with an enthusiastic nod as tears began to roll down her face, and she answered him with a very sassy, "Maybe."

What are the facts?

- There was a flu outbreak in the 1930's that took the lives of many people in the valley.
- The TVA purchased the land that is now Lake Chatuge in the 1940's.
- The sherriff's home really was part of the old jail.
- There was one documented death in Hayesville of a TVA Employee.
- Corundum mines are prevalent in the area.
- The Elf School still stands today just off of the banks of the lake.
- The Copper Door is an amazing restaurant that is ran by world renowned Chef Dennis Barber.
- The Hayesville Historical Society is a wealth of knowledge on the history of Hayesville.

…And the Gold?

Well, people have been searching for that for a long time. The true golden nugget is this amazing town. The views are second to none with a downtown square that is filled with great shops, antiques and restaurants.

1954

&

The Unspoken

Truth

Coming soon...

Made in the USA
Columbia, SC
17 November 2017